Jed's Journal

A GUIDE FOR THOSE LEFT BEHIND

David Mendoza III

BOOKS FOR HIS GLORY
From His Heart to Yours

www.booksforhisglory.com

Jed's Journal
A Guide for those Left Behind

Copyright © 2025 David Mendoza III

All rights reserved. No part of this publication may be reproduced, distributed, or transmitted in any form or by any means, including photocopying, recording, or other electronic or mechanical methods, without the prior written permission of the publisher, except in the case of brief quotations embodied in critical reviews and certain other noncommercial uses permitted by copyright law.

All Scripture quotations, unless otherwise indicated, are taken from the Holy Bible, New International Version®, NIV®. Copyright ©1973, 1978, 1984, 2011 by Biblica, Inc.™ Used by permission of Zondervan. All rights reserved worldwide. www.zondervan.com. The "NIV" and "New International Version" are trademarks registered in the United States Patent and Trademark Office by Biblica, Inc.™

ISBN Hardcover: 979-8-9933809-0-2
ISBN Paperback: 979-8-9922134-5-4
ISBN eBook: 979-8-9933809-1-9

First Edition: October 2025
Edited by Gina Mushynsky

Printed in the United States of America

DEDICATION

To my family, I express my gratitude for your unwavering love and support throughout this journey. To those who are left behind, keep your focus on Jesus, regardless of the circumstances. He is the way, the truth, and the life.

CONTENTS

chapter one

THE PREPARATION

"Be prepared, and keep your lamps lit. Then you will be like servants waiting for their master to return from the wedding banquet, so that when he comes and knocks, they can open the door for him immediately."

LUKE 12:35–36

Ever since I was a young child, I have always felt separated from others. Perhaps it was because I was an only child raised by my grandparents. Nevertheless, I have always sensed a calling on my life for something more significant than just my own existence.

My name is Jedidiah Christopher Baker, but my friends

call me Jed. I grew up in a rural area of east Texas. After my parents tragically passed away in a car accident, my grandparents took me in when I was just five years old.

My grandfather, a Desert Storm veteran, has always been skilled at preparing for the worst. Throughout my upbringing, he taught me a great deal about survival and prepping. He also showed me how to hunt and fish, and most importantly, he instilled in me the value of caring for others and placing them first. On the other hand, my grandma taught me one crucial lesson: to love God above all else.

I had a truly unforgettable childhood, even though I lost my parents when I was very young. My grandparents filled that void in so many ways. I still feel the absence of my parents deeply, and honestly, their memory seems to fade a little more with each passing year. My grandma keeps a photo album of them, which she occasionally shares with me, and that has been a great comfort in preserving their memory.

The night of the tragedy, my parents had just dropped me off at my grandparents' house. If only I had known that would be the last time I would see them, I would have hugged them a little longer or at least talked to them a little more.

It was their special date night, and they had planned a lovely evening out, starting with dinner followed by a late-night movie. On their way back from the theater, a deer suddenly appeared, my dad swerved to avoid it, which caused them to lose control of the car and crash into a tree on the side of the road. They were both taken to the hospital, but unfortunately, they didn't survive.

THE UPBRINGING

Each morning began in a similar way: I had a list of chores to finish before Grandma would prepare breakfast for us. The first thing I would tackle was making my bed, getting dressed, and collecting eggs freshly laid by our chickens. I also needed to feed and water our horses, among other chores.

I will always remember the delightful aroma of crispy bacon, eggs, and coffee coming from my grandma's kitchen. Even though I was too young to enjoy coffee, I loved the smell of it. I can still hear Grandma calling us to come and eat. You've never seen anyone sprint as fast as I did when I heard Grandma's lovely voice calling us home.

Grandpa always sat on the same chair at the dinner table, the one facing the door. Even when we had guests, everyone knew that they should not sit in Grandpa's chair. Another unwritten rule was that no one should eat before Grandpa prayed. As soon as Grandma served us, I automatically knew to close my eyes and bow my head, because Grandpa was about to thank the good Lord for our blessings and provisions.

Grandpa was a man of few words, but when he did speak, it was something special! His words were deep and filled with wisdom, and every single word had significance and intent. I cherished listening to my grandpa: he was the kind of person you could listen to for hours without ever growing tired of his stories and the guidance he offered. I must have heard the gospel countless times, yet each time felt like the very first. My grandparents weren't preachers or evangelists or anything of that sort; they simply lived a life that naturally attracted you to God.

I usually helped my grandma with washing and putting away the dishes right after breakfast. Following that, because we lived in the country, I was homeschooled for most of my early years until I entered high school.

Grandma would begin with a daily Scripture. We would read it together, and then she would clarify its meaning for me. Eventually she started asking me to explain it to her, which I enjoyed very much. Next came history, followed by lessons in math and reading.

After completing my school lessons, I would assist my

grandpa on the farm, doing everything from driving the tractor to mending fences. It was here that I learned invaluable life lessons that you simply can't get in a classroom. I am grateful to God for these times.

Another enjoyable project that Grandpa and I tackled on weekends was building an underground bunker. It took us years to complete, but once we did, every drop of sweat and tear was worth it. I never really asked Grandpa why we were building it; I just instinctively always knew the answer.

HIGH SCHOOL

My grandfather always believed that while homeschooling had its advantages, I shouldn't be sheltered from the outside world. He wanted me to engage with society and understand what it was like to have a social life, and what better environment to do that than high school?

Even though I was the new kid at school, I was already familiar with many of the students there, as we had grown up in the same area and would often run into each other in town when we went out to gather supplies.

My first day was thrilling; to be honest, I felt a bit anxious, but it was enjoyable to be with other students. The first class I attended was history. I had already covered much of the material they were teaching, thanks to my grandma; nonetheless, it served as a great review for me. I discovered that this was a recurring theme throughout the day.

I met so many great people, especially at lunch. A bunch of kids asked me to join their table. They seemed to enjoy a lot of the same things I did. From the start, we really clicked. Richard, David, Alli, Jasmine, and Regi became my closest high school friends. Sure, I made other friends over the years, but this was my main crew. We called ourselves "the A-Team."

In the summer, my grandpa urged me to register for the football tryouts. Interestingly, the coach knew my dad well: They had been good friends and played on the same football team during their high school years.

The first thing Coach Dillon mentioned to me was that I shouldn't expect any special treatment simply because he had been friends with my dad. He made it clear that I would need to earn my place just like everyone else. I was taken aback by this, and my reply to the coach was just a simple "Yes, sir!"

I believe my grandpa truly prepared me for this moment and so much more. Every time we engaged in activities together, whether it was playing football or working on a project, I always sensed that he was imparting lessons that went beyond the immediate task at hand. It felt as though he was sharing invaluable life skills and wisdom that would serve me well in various aspects of my life.

The day of the tryouts had finally arrived. The coaches kicked things off with a bunch of drills and made us run quite a bit. Once they assessed our fitness levels, they had us perform a few plays to catch the ball. The next step involved each of us throwing the ball to showcase our skills. I felt like I did all right, but I wasn't certain if I'd make the team. Regardless of the result, I was just happy to be part of it.

Once the tryouts were wrapped up, they brought us in one by one to tell us if we made the team. When it was my turn, the coach asked me a simple question: "Where have you played before?" I stared at him, puzzled, and replied, "Nowhere, sir." Then he wanted to know where I'd picked up my skills. I told him my grandfather taught me everything I know. The coach scratched his head and simply said, "Welcome to the team, kid! You made it!"

The coach then mentioned that because I was a freshman, he couldn't assign me to the quarterback position. Instead, I would start as a receiver and, if I proved myself, there was a chance I could eventually be moved to quarterback. At that moment, I didn't mind what position I was given; I was simply thrilled to have made the team. I would have been just as content being the water boy for the team.

The months flew by, and before you realized it, the first game of the season arrived. Even though I wasn't scheduled to play that evening, we were all thrilled to be there. My grandparents were eager to attend the game, despite my telling them I wouldn't be playing that night. I didn't mind their attendance at all; I just hoped they wouldn't feel it was a wasteful trip. I cherished my grandparents, as they always supported me in everything I pursued.

I saw that all my friends were present, too, when I glanced over at the bleachers. These wild guys had created all sorts of signs with my name on them, cheering for me, while I sat on the sidelines with the other nonplayers.

As we approached the second half, our team found itself trailing by nine points when something unexpected occurred. The starting receiver got injured badly enough that he couldn't continue playing. Without missing a beat, the coach shouted my name and told me to get ready because I was going in.

I was in disbelief at what I was hearing when the coach shouted my last name for the second time: "Baker, move it! You're in: get ready!" I hadn't expected to play at all that season, especially not on the night of the first game. Regardless, I was thrilled to be part of the game.

I had no idea what God was preparing me for, but I was savoring every moment. On the next play, the coach instructed our quarterback to throw the ball in my direction. Sure enough, the ball came my way. I remember everything happening in slow motion—as soon as I caught the ball, I sprinted like I had never sprinted before. As I headed toward the end zone a few larger players tried to tackle me, but thanks to my days on the farm, I managed to outrun them all. In my mind, I imagined Grandma calling us for breakfast, and I had to get there quickly.

Before I realized it, I was in the end zone—touchdown! The excitement in the air was palpable, especially since we had also scored a field goal and were now tied.

After several plays, we were down to just seconds on the clock. Our team had possession of the ball, and once again, the coach instructed the quarterback to throw it my way. What happened next is a blur; all I remember is one moment the ball was with the quarterback, and the next, I was in the end zone catching the winning touchdown!

LIVING FOR HIM

My high school life changed dramatically after that first football game of the season. Students I didn't even know would come up to me and say hi in the hallways. I truly believe this was a great opportunity to not only make new friends but also share the love of God with others.

My grandmother always taught me that as Christians, we didn't have to force our beliefs on anyone. She told me that when a person truly loves God it would show in their lives, and that love would draw others to Him. I did my best to love the Lord with all my heart. I made mistakes here and there, but I always tried to place Him first in anything and everything I did.

I still remember the day it happened. My grandfather and I were sitting under the big oak tree, taking a break after a hard day's work. I must have been about eleven years old. As we were both looking up to the clear blue sky, my grandpa had been talking about heaven and how wonderful it would be. I vividly remember telling my grandpa that I knew we needed to ask Jesus to be our Savior to get to heaven, but I never really understood how to ask Him into your heart.

In the most loving and patient way, my grandpa looked at me gently and asked, "How did you invite me into your heart, Jed?" At that moment it all made sense: it wasn't about a formula or a three-step method to invite Jesus into your heart; it just occurs naturally. It's a relationship, and like any other relationship, it just takes time to cultivate. Love comes naturally, and when it comes to the Father, He is the one who invites us to Him.

Since that day when my grandpa and I spoke under the oak tree, I knew without a shadow of a doubt that I had Jesus in my heart and that I would never do anything to hurt Him or my grandparents.

Everything I did, whether in the classroom or on the football field, I did with all my heart for God. Don't misunderstand me; I encountered some tough days, but I was confident that as long as I kept pushing forward, everything would turn out fine.

Believe it or not, my school had a worship team that was searching for a guitarist. I had been praying for a chance like this. I loved sports, but this was different: it was something my heart truly desired.

I adored playing the guitar. My grandpa taught me what the old-timers refer to as "cowboy chords." We would play and sing gospel hymns and other worship songs together. Grandma would always join us after the second or third song. Those are beautiful memories I hold dear in my heart. Grandpa would set up a campfire outside, and we would gather around it, singing our hearts out.

As I grew older, my friends from school and I would meet at our farm on weekends to do the same. There was something special about singing and playing around an open campfire, gazing up at the stars, and thanking God for all we had.

Tryouts for the worship team were scheduled right after school. This meant I would miss the bus, and Grandpa would need to come pick me up. When I told him about my audition for the worship team, he immediately reassured me not to worry and just to let him know what time he needed to be there.

When I arrived for the audition, there were two other students trying out with me: George and Grace. I knew George played guitar and was quite good at it, but I had never met Grace before and had no idea about her skills.

George was the first to audition, followed by Grace, and then it was my turn. When I heard Grace play, my heart melted at the beautiful melody she played. Honestly, it felt like my heart was about to burst.

Ms. Rivers, our music teacher, expressed her gratitude to all of us for auditioning, and she said she would inform us the following day about who made the team.

That night, I couldn't sleep at all; I wasn't sure if it was due to my nervousness about whether I had made the team or if it was because I was anxious to see that lovely girl named Grace.

The next day, I hurried as quickly as I could to the music room, but when I arrived, Grace was already there, waiting outside the music teacher's office.

I smiled at her, she smiled back, and I introduced myself, saying, "Hi, I'm Jed, one of the guys who tried out yesterday." Grace laughed and replied, "I know, silly! I was there with you."

Suddenly, the door to the teacher's office swung open and George stepped out, looking disappointed. I thought to myself, if George didn't make it, then I don't have a chance.

Ms. Rivers glanced at both Grace and me, signaling for us to enter her office. I had no idea what was about to happen next. I do remember whispering a small prayer, telling God that no matter what happened, I trusted in Him and wanted His will to be done.

The first words that came from the teacher were, "Congratulations, you made the team."

Grace and I exchanged puzzled looks, then glanced back at Ms. Rivers. The teacher then clarified: "I'm sorry—

congratulations to both of you, you have both secured spots on the worship team."

I questioned Ms. Rivers: How could this be possible when there was only one guitarist spot available? She replied, "Well, if you don't want it, Jed, I'm sure Grace wouldn't mind being the sole guitarist on the team."

"No, ma'am," I quickly interjected, "that's not what I meant. I'm more than happy to play with Grace, I mean, the worship band."

Ms. Rivers appreciated the way Grace and I had performed, so she decided to include both of us in the worship team.

THE INVITATION

My schedule became quite hectic in no time; after all, it was our senior year, and time seemed to pass by so swiftly. I continued to participate in football and various school activities, including the worship team. To add to the excitement, Coach Dillon had me start as quarterback last year. We'd aimed to reach the state finals but fell short, and now he has high hopes for us to go all the way this year.

Honestly, I still found joy in being part of the football team, but my priorities had changed. Grace and I began an after-school Bible study group at the local library. A few of our classmates and I would gather twice a week for fellowship and devotion. I consistently invited my closest friends—the A-Team—and only Richard and Regi had attended a few times. I never stopped inviting them or any of my other friends.

This year felt particularly strange, not just because it was my senior year, but also because there was an unusual vibe in the air that I wasn't alone in sensing. Grace noticed it, and both of my grandparents did too. For some reason, it felt like time had accelerated significantly, and we were racing against the clock.

I constantly felt a deep urgency within me to share the gospel with as many people as possible. For most of my life I had embraced a live and let live philosophy, but after drawing closer to Jesus, I realized I couldn't overlook the fate of those who die without salvation.

The idea that Christ might return soon for His church, leaving many behind simply because they chose to reject Him and weren't ready to live for Him, troubled me greatly. Additionally, the thought of my friends being among those left behind caused me so much distress that I experienced several sleepless nights filled with these concerns.

That's why Grace and I thought it would be a good idea

to start a Bible study group—we figured it could help anyone who had questions about our faith. We really wanted to connect with our fellow students and the community.

Sharing the gospel with my friends has been tough. We've been friends for three years, and during that time, I've tried to share my faith with them. Most of them were open to it, but none of them truly committed their hearts to the Lord. They often say they're happy that religion works for me, but it's just not their thing.

If only they could understand that having a relationship with Jesus isn't about strict rules or forcing changes. If only they could realize that true peace and love can only be found in Him. Plus, without Him, we won't make it to heaven. I'll stick to what my grandma always advised: Love them unconditionally and be a light to them, a friend they can count on no matter what.

I had a whole year before my friends and I went our different ways. Grace and I were gearing up to start at the University of Texas at Tyler next fall, which was both thrilling and a bit bittersweet. It was thrilling because it marked a new chapter in my life, and I was eager to see what God had planned for us. But it was also sad since I wouldn't be hanging out with most of my friends as much anymore: Richard and

Alli had applied to a college out of state, Jasmine and David were set on joining the military, and Regi was going to UT Tyler with us. So yeah, the A-Team was splitting up after our senior year.

I never would have imagined that our senior year would be this hectic. Not only did I have to focus on keeping my grades up and managing my dual enrollment classes, but I also had to deal with all the college prep, applying for scholarships and grants, and filling out all the paperwork that comes with being an academic recipient of a disabled veteran. Because of my grandpa's time in the Marines and my adoption as his son, I got to enjoy the educational benefits. This really took a load off our shoulders when it came to the financial pressure of going to college.

The big night we had all been looking forward to was finally upon us—prom night! The plan was for me to pick up my date, Grace, and meet up with the gang there. As I stood in the doorway of Grace's house, a wave of nervousness hit me. When her parents opened the door, I could barely string two words together; all I managed to say was "Hello!"

Grace's folks were the sweetest people around. Her dad was a pastor, and her mom worked as our local vet. I was so nervous! They welcomed me in and asked how I was doing and if I was excited. All I could manage to say was "Yes!"

Out of nowhere, I spotted Grace coming down the stairs, and she looked angelic! I couldn't believe it was her! She'd always been pretty, but wow—she looked divine! As she made her way down the steps, the only thing I could say was, "Beautiful!"

Her parents turned to me and asked, "Excuse me, did you say something, Jed?"

"Oh, I meant to say she looks beautiful!"

With a big smile, Grace asked, "Are you ready, Jed?"

Man, was I ever ready!

As we were heading out, Grace's dad said, "You kids be careful," and I replied, "Yes sir!" He added, "Please have her back at a decent hour!" I assured him, "Yes sir! I will, definitely!"

When we arrived at the dance, we found the A-Team had saved us two chairs. The venue, an old department store that had been transformed into a space for special events, looked stunning. You wouldn't even have guessed it used to be a department store.

We had an amazing and unforgettable night that we'll treasure for a long time. The food was super good and went beyond what we'd thought it would be.

I brought my guitar and played some tunes that everyone loved. To make things even more fun, the school organized a karaoke session, and the guys really got into it and had a great time! At the end of the night, there was a touching moment when we all hugged, and it hit us that this could be the last time we all came together like this.

chapter two

THE RAPTURE

For the Lord Himself will descend from heaven with a loud command, with the voice of an archangel, and with the trumpet of God, and the dead in Christ will be the first to rise. After that, we who are alive and remain will be caught up together with them in the clouds to meet the Lord in the air. And so we will always be with the Lord.

1 THESSALONIANS 4:16–17

Graduation day had finally arrived, and the excitement in the air was just incredible. This was it: our final day as high school students and the end of a long chapter in our lives. My friends and I had different plans for after high school, but we promised to always support each other no matter what.

Summer was a time for reflection and relaxation before

we took the big step into college. At the farm, it was business as usual; work didn't stop just because it was summer. I continued to help my grandparents in any way I could. I enjoyed lending a hand; it allowed me to appreciate the blessings God had given me.

Grace and I spent a lot of time together that summer. We both understood that even though we would be going to the same college, we each had our own paths to follow and would be quite busy. I was majoring in computer engineering, while she was going into nursing. Our family, her parents and my grandparents, were proud of us.

As for our Bible study group, we kept meeting regularly. Usually, it was the same two or three kids who would show up, but we grew close to one another. Occasionally, someone new would join us. Overall, we loved having these gatherings. They were a huge blessing. Spiritually, we grew more than we ever thought possible. Our relationship with the Lord strengthened with each passing day.

I had a strong desire for my friends to truly embrace the Lord as their Savior. There were moments when I found myself wishing I could somehow compel them to develop a personal relationship with Jesus. However, I knew that this approach was not right. After all, our Lord does not force himself on anyone, so it wouldn't be right for me to do that to anyone else. Yet, despite this understanding, I couldn't help but feel an overwhelming sense of urgency, as if we were racing against the clock.

COLLEGE BOUND

Orientation day turned out to be a fantastic experience! We had the chance to thoroughly explore the entire campus, which was both exciting and informative. I was particularly thrilled to finally see my dorm room, a space that would soon become my home away from home. The whole experience was exhilarating, although I have to confess that it also stirred up a bit of anxiety within me as I navigated this new environment.

Furthermore, I received my class schedule, and I was taken aback by how packed it was. Clearly, I had a busy semester ahead. On a positive note, I was really pleased with my performance in math, especially considering that I had a significant number of math classes lined up.

One of the most cherished aspects of our college experience was the fortunate proximity of Grace's dormitory to mine, which was merely a short stroll away. This convenient distance enabled us to spend time together, greatly enhancing the strength of our friendship. We often engaged in deep conversations about our aspirations and shared dreams of one day getting married after we completed our degrees. However, we both agreed that our current priority should be our studies, and we aimed to fully embrace and enjoy every moment of our college journey.

Before long, we found ourselves having a comfortable routine, and I soon realized that the classes were more challenging than I had initially anticipated. Grace and I put forth our best efforts to keep up with the coursework, and we made it a point to check in with each other from time to time.

Most weekends, we would attend chapel services together, and afterward, we would spend time at the student recreation center, enjoying various activities. During this period, we also made a number of new friends who shared our beliefs, and we cherished moments spent sipping coffee and engaging in casual worship together.

One Sunday morning, we dropped by Grace's old church where her dad was still the pastor. We totally surprised everyone that day, but honestly, the most shocked person was me. Grace's dad had been talking about how important it was to share our testimony with others. Out of the blue, he called me up and asked if I could hop on stage and share my story. Before I knew it, I was up there with a microphone in my hand.

What happened next shocked everyone, including myself. I began by telling everyone that my parents passed away in a car crash when I was just a kid. Then I talked about how, despite missing them deeply, God always looked out for me and blessed me with grandparents who more than filled the void left by my parents. I made it clear that my grandparents could never take the place of my parents, but I was thankful that they were the ones who brought me up.

I told everyone that what the enemy meant for harm, God had turned it around for good. As a kid, I didn't really get why my parents passed away so young, but I never doubted God's plan for my life. I've trusted Him since I could walk, but the moment He became more real to me than ever was one summer day when Grandpa and I were sitting under the big oak tree on our property.

"That day, Jesus felt more real than ever. That was the day I gave my heart to Jesus, or rather, that was the day I surrendered everything to Him. Since that moment, I haven't looked back; sure, there have been tough days, but I know He's the one who carries me through life."

The next words that came out of my mouth surprised everyone, including Grace and her parents; and honestly, I was taken aback too. It felt like someone else was speaking while I just stood there, listening to myself. Out of nowhere, I blurted out, "Because of what God has done in my life, I now know exactly what I want to do with my future. I want to share with the world what He has done for me. I want to serve Him as a preacher and spread the gospel to everyone!"

You could have heard a pin drop. I couldn't tell if Grace's parents were happy, upset, or just plain shocked. Ever since I was a kid, I felt like I had something important to share with the world, but I never thought in a million years that I would want to be a preacher!

PRIORITIES

As we wrapped up our first year in college, everything felt like it was on track. I chose to stick with my major, but I also opted to enroll in some online biblical studies courses. Whenever I shared this with others, they looked at me as if I had completely lost it. They just couldn't grasp why I would want to add that extra workload.

By this point, my priorities had changed. I felt a strong urge to share the message of Jesus with everyone. I never really saw myself as a preacher, but if that was what it took to spread the good news, then I was all in. When I shared my new plan with my grandparents, they were happy. I wasn't sure how they would take it, but they responded even better than I'd expected.

Grace was incredibly supportive. She firmly believed that this was a divine calling, stating that there was no way I would choose to become a preacher on my own without God's influence. Her parents were still processing the news but were also very encouraging. In fact, her dad even offered to help with anything I might need.

We had a brief pause before the next semester kicked off. I decided to make the most of it by working on something I had wanted to do for ages. I had begun a journal quite some time back; it was more than just a journal, though—it was a guide I'd started for my friends in case the Lord's return was quicker than expected, and they were left behind.

Besides my journal, I also wanted to pack a go-bag stocked with supplies and a map, or at least a hint about a map tucked inside. The map had written directions on how to reach the hidden bunker that Grandpa and I constructed. Nobody knew about our bunker, not even Grace. Grandpa said it was wise to keep it a family secret, for good reasons. I felt a bit guilty about not being able to share it with anyone, but I realized that in the end, it was for the best.

As I filled the go-bag, I realized it needed to be lightweight for easy carrying, yet it must include the essentials for surviving a three- to five-day trek (the time it would take to reach our farm from the college). It felt oddly strange to be packing this bag while also writing a letter to my friends, the A-Team.

I began the letter by expressing my love for each of them and how much they meant to me. They all held a unique spot in my heart. Together, we became strong and had been there for one another during the challenging moments of our high school years. School would have been entirely different without them; I viewed them as siblings I had never had. I went on in the letter to ask them, even though it might seem a bit odd, to take my words seriously and listen to what I had to say. I shared that one day, they might wake up to find the world in complete chaos:

> Friends, if one day you wake up and the world is not as it once was, and you discover that millions of people, including myself, have disappeared, please remember what I've warned you about this event. Do not be alarmed; it signifies that Jesus has returned for His church, which Christians refer to as the rapture.
>
> Things will take a turn for the worse; however, I have come up with a plan to ensure your safety during

this challenging period. As for those of us who have vanished, rest assured, we are safe and sound. If everything unfolds as intended, I assure you we will reunite. The most important thing for you to keep in mind right now is that a significant falsehood will be spread regarding those who have vanished, so please do not believe it! Follow the plan I will provide for you and keep your destination a secret from everyone.

Once these disappearances occur, whether it's months or years from now, please stick to the plan right after they happen. Honestly, I'd been feeling this strong urge to warn you, just like I have in person, that the return of the Lord Jesus is near and that the only path to eternal salvation is through Him. He's the only one who has paid the price for our sins. I get that you have a lot of questions about what's going on, and they will all be addressed, but the main focus should be on your salvation.

No matter what comes next, the key thing for you to do right now is to give your heart to the Lord Jesus Christ. Without Jesus, you won't be able to handle the massive deception that's on its way to the world.

Once the vanishings occur, you'll have a brief chance to reach the location I've outlined for you. Keep in mind that there will be complete chaos like you've never experienced, and things will escalate from bad to worse. Nevertheless, stay focused! You need to stay dedicated and keep your mind on the journey.

One final note: A man will emerge from the chaos, appearing to have all the solutions and vowing to deliver peace to everyone. Don't fall for the deception!!! I will provide further details in the journal you will discover when you arrive at my college dorm. Once you reach there, I will have a go-bag waiting for you with the journal inside. Love, Jed!

A NORMAL DAY: RICHARD

The day it happened, everything felt just like any other day. Everything was fine, until ...

We had had our fair share of warnings, but we decided to ignore them. Repeatedly, our friends and family had told us this day would arrive. We chose to follow our own path, and our own path deceived us.

When the disappearances occurred, the first person I thought of was Jed. I immediately tried calling him, but all the lines were busy; I assumed everyone who was still around was trying to reach out to their loved ones. When I couldn't connect with him, I quickly remembered that he had sent me a letter that I hadn't opened yet. I suppose I had been too caught up in my fabricated life that I believed was unbreakable.

As I opened Jed's letter, the very first thing that caught my eye was: "WARNING: YOUR SAFETY DEPENDS ON YOU READING THIS LETTER!" He went on to say:

> Dear Richard,
>
> If you're reading this letter and millions of people have vanished from the planet, it means Jesus has come for His followers. This event is referred to in the Bible as the rapture (1 Thessalonians 4:16–17). Yes, you've been left behind, but it's not too late for you to reach heaven. I won't sugarcoat it; things are going to get rough. The path ahead won't be simple, but if you stay committed, we'll see each other again.

Getting to Jed's dorm was definitely going to be a challenge. The first thing to go after the disappearances was the power, and there were wrecked cars and planes everywhere. As I gazed out my window, I saw people everywhere crying and shouting the names of their loved ones while clutching pieces of clothing that had been left behind.

The scene was an apocalyptic nightmare, with flames raging in every direction, illuminating the chaos that unfolded. Looting reached unprecedented levels, as if a collective madness had taken hold of the crowd. People seemed to have lost all sense of reason, driven solely by their instincts and an overwhelming sense of desperation, as they acted without restraint or consideration for the consequences of their actions.

After a prolonged period of darkness and uncertainty, the power finally returned, illuminating our surroundings once more. As the familiar hum of electricity filled the air, we eagerly turned on the television, tuned in to the radio, and checked our phones, only to be met with a chilling nationwide emergency alert. The message was clear and urgent: We were instructed to make our way to a family processing center, or FPC. Jed had foreseen this scenario; he had previously warned us about the potential dangers of these centers. He had strongly advised us against attending, expressing his concerns about the implications of the mandatory mark that authorities would soon require us to accept. His warnings echoed in my mind as I processed the gravity of the situation.

It's incredible how quickly these FPCs popped up. I

heard they transformed a lot of the shopping centers we used to visit all the time. Most of these shopping centers were perfectly situated in our neighborhoods, almost like they were planned that way.

The first message that was disseminated, apart from the direction for us to report to an FPC, conveyed that the government was diligently pursuing an investigation into the circumstances surrounding all the individuals who had gone missing. They further reassured the public that the truth regarding these disappearances would ultimately be revealed, and that those who were accountable would be held responsible for their actions. Moreover, they emphasized the importance of individuals reporting to a local FPC, as this would facilitate proper accounting and registration of those affected.

I made sure to pack only the essentials and set off toward Jed's dorm room. Choosing to ride my bike instead of driving a car turned out to be a great decision; my motorcycle allowed me to zoom through the chaotic highway traffic with ease. *It's astonishing,* I thought, *how our lives have completely transformed in such a short period.* The speed at which everything was changing was truly remarkable.

TOTAL CHAOS

Checkpoints were set up all over the place, staffed by a new police force called the One World Federation Police (OWFP). In the midst of the chaos, global leaders came together to form a unified police force to help keep peace, among other things. The primary goal of these checkpoints was straightforward: to verify if someone had checked in with an FPC and received their mark.

It had only been a couple of weeks, and this guy known to everyone as John Paul Cohen had already emerged from the chaos to advocate for peace among the nations. Everything he said and promised sounded great ... almost too good to be true, in my opinion. If it weren't for Jed's letter cautioning me about him, I might have easily been deceived by his falsehoods.

As I headed to Jed's dorm, I had plenty of time to think about everything happening around me. What should have been a simple four-hour trip turned into something much longer. The roads I was on looked different, scattered with debris and packed with people who were stuck, unable to find their way through the mess. The OWFP was out there making rounds, picking up anyone they could find that did not have a mark. I had a few encounters with them while driving, but I was thankful for my familiarity with the back roads and shortcuts, which made it easier to navigate through the chaos and avoid the OWFP.

It didn't take long for me to realize that it seemed as though everything had been meticulously orchestrated in advance. The rapid pace of events, from the swift mobilization of the FPCs and the OWFP, to the sudden rise of this individual named Cohen who seized complete control not only of the United States but also of every nation around the globe, indicated that this was far from a mere coincidence. This was a clear demonstration of exceptional strategic planning at the highest level.

Without realizing it, we had gradually become desensitized, primed for someone to take full control over our lives. We had been conditioned to yearn for a savior—not for the salvation of our souls, but for the very essence of our existence. Over time, we were transformed into beings that were completely dependent on others or external influences. This dependency extended to every aspect of our lives, from the food we ate and the entertainment we sought to the ways we engaged with technology and interacted with one another.

Our dependence on them grew to an absolute level; we were ensnared by their falsehoods. The pieces have finally fallen into place—when society becomes wholly dependent on a specific thing or person, it creates a perfect opportunity for that entity to remove all the essentials they rely on, making them even more dependent. This is the role of the mark; without it, one cannot participate in buying, selling, or even existing. It's the ultimate mechanism of control.

What is truly remarkable about this entire situation is that Jed had actually given us a heads-up years ago. Everyone loved Jed; he had this magnetic quality that drew people in. However, we often thought he was a little eccentric, just another person caught up in wild conspiracy theories. How wrong we were! In hindsight, we should have taken his warnings seriously when we had the chance.

I definitely know one thing: I'm going to start paying attention and follow everything he's laid out for us. This commitment starts right now. However, before I dive in, I've made the decision to take a step that I should have taken a long time ago.

Reflecting on my past, I find myself questioning why I never fully devoted my life to the Lord. Perhaps I was under the impression that there would always be a tomorrow to make that choice. I did appreciate the few Bible studies I attended with Jed and Grace, but once again, I think I was caught in the belief that I had all the time in the world to embrace Christ.

I quickly pulled over to the side of the road, and right then and there, I asked the Lord to forgive me for all my sins. I requested that He create a new heart in me that would love Him and know His ways. I asked Him to forgive my selfishness and for living life on my own terms. I sought His strength for the journey I was on and guidance to lead me in the right direction. I also asked if He could use someone like me to help bring others to Him during these chaotic times, that I was willing. Finally, I thanked Him for Jed and everything he had done.

chapter three

JED'S JOURNAL

"Peace I leave with you; My peace I give to you. I do not give to you as the world gives. Do not let your hearts be troubled; do not be afraid."

JOHN 14:27

Getting to Jed's dorm was quite a challenge. What was supposed to be a four-hour trip ended up taking eight hours. This was largely due to the need to steer clear of the OWFP. The media portrayed this group as having nothing but our best interests at heart. Their message was filled with promises of safety and care on behalf of the "One World Global Order" (OWGO). This was the title of the newly established global government headed by the newly elected global president, John Paul Cohen. Yet, I was aware of the truth.

As I attended college, I worked part-time at a technology firm that focused on the design and production of microchips for various technological applications. Among the many projects I was involved in, one particularly troubled me. The company was tasked with creating a smart chip that incorporated artificial intelligence technology. My unease arose from the knowledge that this chip was meant for human use, rather than being solely for devices. I found myself questioning the ethical implications and potential risks associated with integrating AI into a product intended for direct human interaction.

I had never encountered such advanced technology in my entire life. The little I managed to learn about the AI chip, also known as the forerunner chip, frightened me. With this chip, individuals would no longer require keys to unlock their homes or start their cars; they wouldn't even need a wallet or cash, and identity theft would become a thing of the past. This was merely the tip of the iceberg regarding its capabilities. The unsettling aspect of the AI technology within this chip was that it was believed to learn about its user. Not just learning but also adapting and enhancing its surroundings.

The team of developers responsible for the forerunner chip had already conducted tests on primates, and the results were completely successful. The chip performed far better than they had anticipated. Within a year, it had undergone testing and received approval for human trials. The forerunner chip was extraordinary; its ability to adapt to the human body was astonishing. Once implanted, it would automatically begin scanning from the inside out, capable of identifying any irregularities. For instance, if a subject had a cold or any illness, it would instantly start emitting frequencies to counteract it, allowing the subject to recover almost immediately.

The forerunner chip was truly remarkable, to the extent that every employee had to sign a confidentiality agreement to protect its secrets. Following extensive testing, it was found that even participants suffering from cancer exhibited notable improvements in their condition. Additionally, individuals diagnosed with dementia also reported enhancements in their cognitive functions, highlighting the chip's potential benefits across various health issues.

In my final days working there, I discovered that this chip functioned like a second brain, allowing users to download endless information onto it, while the human brain would draw from the chip just like a computer accesses an external hard drive. Not only would it draw from this source, but it would also actually store this information, effectively educating its user in any area they desired, thereby significantly boosting their intelligence.

What frightened me the most is that this was precisely the chip that Jed had warned us about, and it was now being employed as a form of identification. I could hardly fathom the potential uses it might have under the control of the OWGO.

IF YOU'RE READING THIS

I finally arrived at Jed's college, and honestly, the outside felt like a ghost town. I hurried over to his dorm room, and when I got there, the door was cracked open. I cautiously pushed the door open, and guess who was inside waiting for me? Nope, not the OWFP, but the rest of the A-Team: David, Alli, and Jasmine!

Wow, I was really happy to see them! I wasn't sure if David and Jasmine would show up, since they had joined the military. I gave everyone a huge hug and told them how thrilled I was that they came. David brought up that the military had been disbanded and that only a small part of each branch was taken into the OWFP.

I asked whether they had seen Regi, and right away they answered that she had been part of the disappearances. I questioned their certainty, and David assured me that he was positive she was part of it, as he had recently gotten a letter from her sharing her good news—she had dedicated her life to Jesus. She mentioned that she had been going to chapel with Jed and Grace, and during one of the services, she made the decision to fully commit her life to Christ.

David went on, "I called her right after I read her letter, and she just kept sharing her salvation story with me. She sounded really happy and thrilled. She mentioned that she had never experienced such peace and love in her entire life. Regi was trying to persuade me to dedicate my life to Christ, but for some reason, I told her I wasn't ready. What was I thinking! Now I understand, but it's too late."

I told David that it's not too late to give his heart to Jesus. "Yeah, we missed the first train, but don't forget what Jed said in his letter. We might have missed the rapture, but we can still get to heaven!"

In that moment, David shut his eyes and declared, "I'm ready," with Alli and Jasmine following right behind him. I felt so grateful to have seen this. I closed my eyes too and prayed alongside them. It goes without saying, the A-Team was headed to heaven! But first, we needed to reach the spot Jed had mapped out for us.

Alli then said, "I'm not sure about you all, but I think we need to move fast because the OWFP is going door to door looking for survivors—especially those without the mark.

"Since I was the first to reach the dorm, I spotted the backpack Jed had left for us, and inside was his journal. I began to read it, but I thought it would be better to wait for you all so we could read it together.

"We opened the journal together, filled with excitement as we began to read it. Good old Jed: always with his funny way of lifting your spirits, no matter what the situation was.

"As we flipped through the journal, the first thing that caught our eye was: 'Hey everyone, if you're reading this, it means I've finally reached the end zone! But don't stress, I've got a plan that will definitely lead you to the promised land, and one day we'll reunite.'

" 'As you have seen for yourselves, the rapture has finally happened. Nobody thought it would, but it did! By now, I'm certain the world is in complete chaos, and it won't be long before the man with the plan appears, referred to as the anti-Christ or the son of perdition (2 Thessalonians 2:3–4).

" 'I've packed two kinds of maps in the go-bag, plus a compass. There's a Bible, which serves as a guide for your soul, and a traditional map for your safety. Now, about your safety—first off, you should ditch your phones or anything with a chip. This way, no one can track you.

" 'The next thing you should understand is DO NOT FALL FOR THE DECEPTION! The media will release a statement about the missing individuals. They will attempt to attribute it to UFOs and an alien agenda. Keep in mind what I have previously shared with you: There are no aliens; these are actually demonic entities (fallen angels) masquerading as extraterrestrials. Satan is an expert at disguise (2 Corinthians 11:14).

" 'If it hasn't happened yet, it will be happening soon. They are going to start introducing the mark of the beast (Revelation 13:16). This mark will be placed on your right hand or forehead, and it will help bring about a cashless society. But the scariest part about this mark is that if you choose to accept it, you're making a spiritual commitment to Satan. The mark of the beast represents a total surrender to him; by taking the mark, you are consciously rejecting Christ for eternity and giving full control to the beast system.

" 'Before you begin on the journey, there's one last

thing you should know. Don't let yourself get caught by the global police force, which I bet will spring into action soon after the disappearances. Their main goal will be to catch anyone who refuses the mark, which basically means they're targeting Christians. If they do catch you, they'll offer you a choice: Deny Christ and take the mark, or face beheading (Revelation 20:4). The way this group will treat Christians will be so wicked and vile that I can't share all the details in this journal.'

THE PLAN

" 'Before we dive into the plan I've prepared for you, I need to talk about something even more crucial—the plan of salvation. You all have steered clear of this topic whenever I mentioned it. I think it's time for you to really think about your eternal future. So let's have a little Bible study right now, since I have your attention.

" 'We all come into this world with sin; no one is truly good (Romans 3:23). Because of the actions of Adam and Eve, we are all impacted by this (Romans 5:12–19). Anyone who dies without having their sins forgiven will face eternal damnation in hell (Romans 6:23). Yet God has provided a way for us to avoid hell: He sent His only begotten Son to take our place on the cross for our sins (Romans 5:8). If you openly declare that 'Jesus is Lord' and genuinely believe in your heart that God raised Him from the dead, you will be saved (Romans 10:9). Once you accept this and embrace what Jesus has done for you, there is no longer any condemnation for those who are in Christ Jesus (Romans 8:1). You become a new creation in Christ; the old has gone, and the new is here (2 Corinthians 5:17).

" 'Congratulations, guys! Welcome to the family! If you had already embraced Christ as your Savior prior to our little Bible study, then no worries; it's a great review for you. I really wish I could have been there to see the A-Team come to Christ. But it's all right; at least I'll be able to witness all the angels in heaven celebrating over your salvation, and we'll definitely have a chance to discuss it when we reunite. So let's start with the reason we're all gathered here.

" 'As you travel, be cautious about who you trust, particularly those who bear the mark; people will betray one another to the point of death (Mathew 10:21). I've packed some protein bars and water purification tablets for you to use with river water. You shouldn't need to make any stops at stores for food, not that you could even if you wanted to, since without the mark you can't purchase anything.

" 'I hope you won't have to use it, but just in case, I've stashed a crossbow in the closet, along with a machete and my grandpa's handgun in the go-bag. It's always better to have these things and not need them than to need them and not have them. You'll also find a first aid kit, a flashlight, a crank radio, and a couple of emergency blankets in the bag.

" 'This journey is going to be quite tough, but don't worry, God's got your back. I've charted all the backcountry routes, so avoid the main roads! Throughout the trip, I've also set up some refueling spots where I've hidden water and Meals Ready to Eat for you; don't ask. These supplies are tucked away in different strategic locations along the route.

" 'Usually this journey would take around two hours by car, but since I'm uncertain if the cars will be working, plus I suspect there will be checkpoints on the main roads, you'll need to trek this one on foot. It should take you roughly two to three days if all goes well.

" 'Start by heading to the back of the college. Walk a few clicks southeast until you hit the river. Stick to the river's path in that same direction for about a day and a half. After that, keep going east until you spot a hill—you can't miss it, I've got it all mapped out for you. Once you get past the hill, follow the connecting river for another day and a half, and that will lead you right to our property.

" 'When you get to our place, be sure to enter through the back of the property, near the old barn. Before you go into the barn, make sure no one's tailing you or knows you're there. Once you're inside, you'll find a secret trapdoor under Grandpa's worktable. To get to this trapdoor, you'll need a key that's hanging near the horse stable. Just a heads-up, this key can be tricky to spot; it's cleverly tucked away behind a horseshoe on the wall.

" 'Once you're sure it's safe to head in, just watch out for another locked door at the bottom of the stairs. You'll find the key tucked under the last stair. This will lead you into the bunker that Grandpa and I spent years building. Back then, I didn't really get why Grandpa was so determined to work on it, but now it all makes sense.

" 'We built the bunker to accommodate eight people, so there should be more than enough room. Inside, you'll find essentials to last for seven years. I never understood why my Grandpa kept enough supplies for seven years until I read the book of Daniel.

" 'Don't worry, guys, you've got this! I've added some footnotes for the map and included some Scripture to help you and bring you comfort as you go. Make sure to look out for each other and encourage one another. You can get through this together. I believe in you, and most importantly, I trust that our Lord will keep you safe and see you through.' "

THE ROUTE

It all began as planned; we started our journey with high hopes. We were fortunate enough to gather additional clothing, gear, and provisions from the abandoned dormitories. This place, which had once been a lively center for nurturing young minds for many years, now lay eerily empty and desolate. Little did we know that we were completely unaware of the events that were soon to unfold.

We managed to find the river that Jed had mapped for us. None of us saw what was coming though. The weather was on our side at first; it wasn't too chilly or too warm, but we did encounter some rain now and then, which made things a bit trickier. As we strolled by the riverbank, we spotted some fresh footprints. We figured it would be smarter to keep our distance from the river rather than walk right next to it.

David and Jasmine were pros at this; we had been walking for hours, yet they appeared totally unfazed. Meanwhile, Alli and I had to take breaks, needing to rest about every thirty minutes. I suppose their military training really prepared them for this.

Night fell quickly, so we chose to settle down for the night. We stumbled upon a large fallen oak tree that served as a perfect resting spot. We agreed to take turns sleeping in shifts. The nights were pretty cold; I was really thankful Jed had left us those emergency blankets. He also provided a fire starter stick, which I was glad I knew how to use from my Boy Scout days. Those supplies made a huge difference, but we had to be cautious; we couldn't just light a fire whenever we wanted, as it could attract not only wildlife but also some unwanted visitors.

We figured out how to keep a fire going without smoke by using something called a Dakota fire pit. You dig a main hole and connect it to one or two smaller holes, called feeder holes, about a foot away. When you light the fire in the main hole, the side holes pull in air to the fire's base, increasing the oxygen supply and helping it burn better.

The weather changed drastically overnight, and things took a turn for the worse. While we had been accustomed to feeling tremors in our area, we had never experienced an earthquake stronger than a magnitude 5.0 until today. The intensity of the quake was unlike anything we had ever felt before. Trees were uprooted and scattered everywhere, leaving the land in shambles. Yet the worst was yet to come; shortly after the earthquake, a tremendous group of meteorites rained down around us, igniting fires in all directions.

The circumstances were dire and alarming. Not long after, all the animals started to die off. This led to a significant reduction in food supplies for everyone in the area. As a result, groups of ruthless individuals banded together, resorting to the unimaginable act of hunting other humans for sustenance.

The OWFP saw a crucial opportunity and quickly embraced drone technology; with these drones, they spread a message that turned out to be deceptive and full of false hope. They knew that many survivors were still around, and they worked hard to entice these people to step forward and accept the mark. They offered promises of safety and security, claiming that their only goal was to assist and look after us.

We figured out how to stay out of sight from the drones and not get caught. Everything around us really took a turn for the worse. What was meant to be a three-day hike ended up stretching into days, then weeks, and eventually months.

SAFE ZONE

David not only had picked up self-defense skills during his military service, but he also became a black belt martial arts instructor. While we were out in the wilderness, given all that was happening around us, he shared all his knowledge, which proved to be super useful in our predicament. Besides teaching us martial arts, he and Jasmine also instructed us in marksmanship. It goes without saying: The A-Team had turned into a force to be reckoned with.

From the beginning, we formulated a plan: Should anything happen to one of us, or if we found ourselves apart, we would regroup at the foot of the hill. This spot remained a stronghold, unwavering in the face of the surrounding chaos, and we referred to it as our safe zone.

It occurred at the most unexpected moment. We had become careless in keeping our path clear; and one evening, as we strolled along an old trail, Alli tumbled into a pitfall trap. We realized we had only a limited time to rescue her from that hole before the group responsible for the trap arrived.

Indeed, just as we were in the process of saving her, a band of men approached us. Jasmine skillfully halted a few of them with our crossbow. Meanwhile, David had cleverly concealed himself, biding his time until the perfect moment to launch a flank attack that successfully sent a couple of them tumbling into their own pitfall trap.

At that point, we successfully freed Alli from the trap.

The timing couldn't have been better: We were just about to face the remaining men, who were armed with knives and sticks. Thanks to David's martial arts training, we not only managed to disarm them but also completely kick their butts.

We ran away from those guys so fast that we ended up totally worn out. After that scary experience, we figured it was super important to focus not just on the road ahead but also to cover our tracks. I really think those men we met would do whatever it takes to find us.

Finding food was becoming increasingly tough. We quickly finished the protein bars Jed had packed for us. As for the refueling stations he set up, we managed to locate the first two without any issues. But after the earthquake and the fires, the landscape was shifting, making it harder to spot the stations.

Despite everything, we kept pressing toward Jed's family farm. During our breaks, we made it a habit to not just take turns on lookout duty but also read a chapter from the Bible that was packed in the go-bag. Over the months we traveled, we gained so much knowledge. We began with the New Testament, and the more we read, the more we wished we had embraced the Lord earlier. Now we really got why Jed was so eager to share the gospel with us. It must have been tough for him when we turned down his invitation.

The words we found in the Bible brought us a lot of comfort, so that even when everything around us was falling apart, our hearts stayed strong. We were grateful to our Lord for using Jed and for never giving up on us. While we couldn't return to the past, we could look forward with confidence that, as Jed has often said, one day we will be reunited with him and all our friends and family who have passed on and are now with the Lord.

As we leisurely walked along the path, Jasmine's keen eyes caught sight of an old hunting cabin nestled among the trees. Intrigued, we decided to investigate further, starting with a thorough check to see if the cabin was indeed abandoned. We were cautious, remaining vigilant for any potential booby traps that might have been set up to deter intruders. After ensuring that the area was secure and safe for exploration, we eagerly stepped inside the cabin. To our surprise, we were all struck by how remarkably well-preserved the interior was, as if time had stood still within those walls.

We were convinced that no one had visited in years, yet it appeared pristine. It offered every amenity one could desire. The first thing the girls did was rush to claim the shower for themselves. There were even additional fresh clothes (in camouflage, of course) for both men and women. This was undoubtedly a blessing from the Lord; we had been praying for a place like this, and here it was, right before our eyes.

David naturally made his way to the pantry, and as soon as he opened the door, he was met with a variety of canned goods and large water containers. We hit the jackpot! While the girls took turns in the shower and David was enjoying the food, I stumbled upon a closet filled with weapons and ammo. It had all kinds of guns, from handguns to rifles and even a shotgun. What a score!

We chose to spend the night there, but we were aware that we couldn't linger for too long. We had a great time that evening; we even managed to read a few chapters from the Bible, and just when we thought it couldn't get any better, I stumbled upon some coffee—yes, coffee! It was hidden away in the pantry. Wow, it was delicious! It was a moment we hadn't savored in a long time.

I came across a military-style footlocker next to the bed. Inside, we discovered a paper map of the whole area, an emergency hand radio linked to a headset, some walkie-talkies, and a few other things, including fresh batteries.

The day after we got all our gear ready, we figured it was time to head out. We had heard on the radio that the OWFP was now giving a reward to anyone who could catch and hand over an unmarked person. From then on, they started calling us the "unmarked."

chapter four

DECEPTION

The coming of the lawless one is according to the working of Satan, with all power, signs, and lying wonders, and with all unrighteous deception among those who perish, because they did not receive the love of the truth, that they might be saved.

2 THESSALONIANS 2:9–10

The deception did not occur overnight; our hearts had been prepared to receive the lie that was being spread by the OWGO. Had we not accepted Jesus as our Savior, we too would have fallen for the lie, just like everyone else.

For many years we were misled by the media, politicians, our education system, and social media, creating a scenario where what was right was perceived as wrong and wrong as right. We accepted these lies, almost craving them, similar to the boiling frog effect—going along with it all without a second thought. Little did we know this was all paving the way for the rise of a one-world government led by a single global leader.

The world seemed ready to embrace this false savior, needing just one final push to fully accept him. In a time when chaos reigned supreme and hope had all but disappeared, he presented a distorted vision of hope and a facade of normalcy that many were eager to grasp.

THE WOUND

We referred to them as the others: the Constitutionalists. They were a non-Christian, anti-government faction that despised everything associated with governance. This was the group that conspired to assassinate the global president, John Paul Cohen. As a result of their actions, resistance against the OWGO intensified.

With each passing day, the number of those opposing us grew, creating a sense of entrapment for us believers. It felt as though we were caught in an impossible situation wedged between two formidable forces. On one side, the OWFP was unyielding in their pursuit, relentlessly hunting us down. On the other hand, the increasing numbers of the others were convinced that it was a fight for survival, believing it was either us or them. They were determined to coerce us into joining their ranks, leaving us with no easy way out.

Just when it seemed that the Constitutionalists were gaining ground in their campaign against the OWGO, a shocking event took place. We received the news over the radio: Global president Cohen has been the target of an assassination attack. Tragically, our beloved president had been shot in the head and succumbed to his injuries!

The media reported a deep and overwhelming sense of disbelief and grief among the people. The sole person who possessed all the answers, the one who represented our hopes for a better tomorrow, has now left us forever!

Wait, what? Was he really gone? We were completely unable to comprehend this shocking news. Was it truly over? Will the OWGO be disbanded as a result? Immediately, I remembered that Jed had left behind some notes in his journal that might shed light on the situation.

As we read through the journal, we found it right there, in huge bold letters: "DO NOT BE DECEIVED! The one world leader will be killed and die; but he will rise again, or come back to life (Revelation 13:3). Satan is a deceiver, and the anti-Christ will attempt to imitate Jesus's death and resurrection, all to win the world's approval." How did Jed know this was going to happen? If he hadn't warned us, we would have fallen for the lie too.

Suddenly, while we were still reading the journal, the next thing that came on the radio was, "HE IS ALIVE!"

Wait, what? They weren't referring to Jesus; they were talking about global president Cohen. The media kept claiming it was a miracle.

The atmosphere across the globe overflowed with happiness! People from all walks of life were immersed in festivities and celebrations. This monumental occasion ushered in the transformation that Cohen had long anticipated. To everyone's surprise, many who previously backed the opposing side began to reconsider their stance. Following the remarkable healing that took place, crowds of individuals flocked to express their support for President Cohen.

Cohen's power grew quickly after this, to the extent that he not only announced a single global currency but also a unified world religion. He claimed that all religions had been responsible for hate and wars. To eliminate this issue, he aimed to merge all faiths into one. Shortly after, he appointed a religious figure known only as the Overseer, who was tasked with spreading Cohen's singular message to humanity. All other religions were eliminated, and every religious text, including the Holy Bible, was banned and destroyed.

As soon as we got the news, we rushed to Jed's journal, and once more we saw that he had cautioned us about this Overseer, the False Prophet mentioned in Revelation 13:11–17. There were countless other things our buddy Jed had alerted us to and clarified for us—all the events unfolding right in front of us.

Right after the assassination attempt, it seemed as though the Constitutionalists had completely disappeared from the scene. However, this was not the primary concern Cohen was dealing with at the time. Out of nowhere, thousands of Jewish men started to fervently share the teachings of our Lord Jesus Christ all around the world. Their enthusiasm and determination made them seem invincible, as if they were under some sort of divine protection.

SIGNS AND WONDERS

Cohen became aware that a group of Jews was successfully winning over many people to Christ, which prompted him to escalate the deception. Through a worldwide media broadcast, he proclaimed that the truth had finally come to light. He asserted that all the individuals who had gone missing were actually the evil Christians. He accused the Christian message of being nothing more than hate speech mixed with falsehoods and hostility, and claimed that this was the reason they had been eradicated from existence by our allies, the light bearers.

He took advantage of the moment and declared that there were still individuals present who had accepted the message of Christianity, labeling them as the real adversaries. He asserted that these unmarked individuals aimed to undermine the peace he had diligently established and therefore needed to be eliminated at any cost. The following segment of his speech truly astonished everyone, leaving no room for doubt about his words.

Cohen introduced his loyal assistant, the Overseer, confidently declaring that they were the only ones capable of resolving this problem definitively. To demonstrate their unique abilities, the Overseer began to pray in a language that was foreign to the crowd, invoking flames from the sky. The audience was left in a state of both terror and wonder at the extraordinary display they had just experienced.

Throughout our journey, we were inundated with a relentless stream of distressing news that felt almost unbearable, yet we knew we had to continue moving forward.

Just when we thought the situation couldn't possibly worsen, we were confronted with an even graver reality.

In his relentless pursuit of absolute power and his ambition to maintain a one world religion, he issued a decree that all sacrifices at the Jewish temple must cease. However, the most shocking event was yet to come: While in Jerusalem, Cohen shamelessly entered the temple and committed an act that was beyond comprehension—he sacrificed a pig within the sacred space and audaciously declared himself to be God, all while broadcasting it live for the world to see.

People were in disbelief over what they had just seen. They were uncertain about how to process this. The Overseer quickly praised Cohen in front of the crowd and once more summoned fire from the heavens, proclaiming that Cohen is the one and only true God, here to deliver us.

We realized it was only a matter of time before the OWFP would catch up to us. Even with that threat hanging over us, we kept pushing forward on our journey.

While navigating through the thick forest, we unexpectedly noticed two figures crouched behind a tree. Without a second thought, we swiftly got into a defensive stance, prepared to evaluate the situation and figure out who they were. As we looked at them more intently, we realized they were just two young, frightened teens, obviously lost and in distress.

Coming closer, we could clearly see that they were trying hard to stay out of sight. Their thin faces and hollow eyes hinted that they were really starving, almost like they hadn't eaten a decent meal in ages. Holding on to a snack we had brought from the cabin, we carefully walked up to them. To our surprise, they reached out right away and happily took the food we offered.

Alli swiftly moved to reassure them, gently stating that everything was fine and that we had no intention of hurting them. She then asked if they were alone, to which they both nodded in affirmation while continuing to enjoy their snack. Alli followed up by asking their names, and they introduced themselves as Sarah and Jeremiah.

They appeared to be approximately fourteen or fifteen years old. When we inquired whether they were siblings, they clarified that they were not; rather, they had simply been neighbors prior to the events of the disappearances.

Sarah talked about how her parents had vanished and left her all by herself when it went down. She mentioned that she rushed over to Jeremiah's place because she was at a loss for what to do. Jeremiah shared that his family—parents and brother—were all Christians and had often told him about the rapture, but he never really thought it would occur. With tears in his eyes, he went on to express that he had believed he had plenty of time before fully dedicating his life to Christ.

David wrapped him in a warm bear hug and reassured him, saying, "Don't worry, little brother, we've all been in your shoes. We all thought we had more time; every one of us received warnings, yet we didn't think it would actually come to pass either.

"It's not too late to invite Him into your life. If you're open to it, we can join in prayer with you and Sarah to accept Christ as your Savior. This decision will guarantee that regardless of what life throws our way, we will be heaven bound." Both nodded in agreement, showing their willingness to take this important step.

THE TWO WITNESSES

Sarah wondered if they could join us, since they had nowhere else to go and things were getting pretty rough out there. Without a second thought, we all said yes to them coming along, but we made it clear that we had our own way of doing things. If they were willing to learn, they were welcome to tag along.

We continued walking until suddenly another earthquake hit, and this one was even stronger than the last. It felt like there was nowhere to escape to, so we gathered in a huddle and prayed aloud for safety. Once the shaking ceased, we looked ahead and noticed that the ground had split open, creating a large gap right in the path we needed to take.

We had just two options: we could either head west or east, since going straight ahead was not an option. We chose to go east, hoping that following the opening to the end wouldn't lead us too far off track.

After days of relentless walking, we were completely worn out. The lack of a proper night's sleep had taken its toll on us, and we desperately needed some water and food. If there was any chance at all to do so, we craved a chance to recharge our tired bodies. Just when we were on the verge of giving in for the night, we came across a deer blind. To our surprise, it turned out to be quite nice, giving us a spark of hope in the midst of our exhaustion.

David and Alli climbed up while we stayed at the bottom, keeping an eye out. Once they reached the top, all we could hear was them shouting, "Jackpot!" They called down to us, saying, "Guys, it's clear—come on up. There's plenty of space for everyone."

When we finally made it up there, it was clear that whoever constructed that blind had done so with comfort in mind. It was designed for four people, yet all six of us managed to fit inside just fine. As we scanned the area for anything useful, we stumbled upon some canned goods, beef jerky, and water! Thank you, Lord! That was precisely what we needed.

From up high you could see for miles, and as we scanned the area, all we could see was destruction everywhere. But that wasn't the worst part; what we saw next truly made our hearts drop. When we looked to the east and west, it appeared that the opening in the ground stretched on for miles in both directions.

We decided to trust in God. We could not walk by what we were seeing, we had to trust that He would help us get home. Then we checked out the map Jed had left us, and it seemed like we were about a third of the way there. It had taken us more than a year to reach this point, and at the rate things were going it might take us a few more months, but only time would reveal the truth.

That night, we followed our usual routine of taking turns to catch some sleep. While one of us stayed alert and kept watch, the others could crash out. We made sure to let Sarah and Jeremiah get their much-needed rest, as it was evident that they hadn't experienced a proper night's sleep in a long time—perhaps even years.

The following morning, we woke up feeling rejuvenated and eager to tackle whatever came our way. We chose to trail to the side of the opening, keeping a safe distance. It felt like we had walked for days, maybe even weeks, until we finally reached the end of the gap caused by the earthquake. This led us to what appeared to be a deserted city.

We strolled between two towering buildings, keeping an eye on our surroundings. By then, night had begun to set in. We figured it would be wise to find a place to stay for the night.

As we entered the building, it felt like someone was keeping an eye on us, so we assigned two watchmen instead of just one. Before we settled down for the night, Jasmine chose to switch on the radio to catch up on what was happening outside.

We were completely caught off guard by what we heard next. It turns out that two mysterious men appeared seemingly out of thin air, clad in ancient robes reminiscent of a bygone era. These individuals were not merely declaring the Word of God to the crowd; they also boldly confronted the OWFP. In fact, there was a shocking report that when the OWFP began to encircle them, these mysterious figures unleashed fire through their mouths upon the vehicles of the OWFP, creating a scene of chaos and disbelief.

This experience seemed as though it was plucked straight from the pages of a biblical story found in the Old Testament. Accounts of their appearances had significantly increased, sparking widespread intrigue and speculation. Additionally, there was a prevailing belief among some that these sightings could be linked to the return of the Prophet Elijah and Enoch, who were thought to be coming back to fulfill their divine mission as described in Revelation 11:1–14.

We were excited to hear this great and terrifying news. For those who were marked, this revelation represented the most dreadful news they could possibly receive. However, for us, it served only to reinforce and solidify our conviction that the Word of God is undeniably true. Regardless of how chaotic or troubling circumstances may have seemed on the surface, we firmly believed that He is always in control.

FRIENDS OR FOES

That night, I struggled to get to sleep. I'm uncertain whether it was due to the news we had received or if I still had the sensation that someone or something was watching us. As we left the building, we heard a soft voice from the adjacent room asking, "Are you friend or foe?"

We quickly concealed ourselves as I replied, "It depends!"

The soft voice then inquired, "What does it depend on?"

I replied, "It depends on whether you are marked or unmarked. We are unmarked; how about you all?" David then interjected, "If you are genuinely unmarked, step out with your hands raised and reveal yourselves." The next thing we observed was a young couple emerging from behind the door's entrance.

There were a ton of questions for them; it seemed like they hadn't seen daylight in ages. The first thing we asked was if anyone else was with them, and they replied, "No, just us. We were part of a larger group, but most of them were taken by the Constitutionalists or the OWFP. We managed to hide inside the walls of this building and discovered a passage through the boiler room."

"What about food?" David replied. "What did you all do for food?"

The young man answered, "We managed to find some here and there in this abandoned building. We still have a bit left, but in a couple of days, we'll be out. By the way, my name is Josh, and this is my wife, Mary."

We quickly introduced ourselves and asked if they could share a little food. Josh offered us some. Then Mary asked where we were headed. After hearing our story, they wanted to know if they could join us. I looked at my partners for a nod of approval and said they could, but I warned them that we still had quite a journey ahead and that it wouldn't be easy.

On our way out, we managed to go around the opening in the ground through the city and made our way back northwest until we found the correct path again. This detour extended our journey by nearly a month. However, if it hadn't been for the earthquake and the ground opening, we wouldn't have met Mary and Josh. So, in the end, it turned out to be a positive experience after all.

Significant strides had been made on the journey. We were exhausted but felt sure that we were nearing Jed's family property. We could hardly contain our excitement; it felt like this would be our little slice of paradise, the promised land, and all thanks to the grace of God.

It felt great to be back on the correct path. The most exciting part was that Jed's map indicated we were not too far from one of his refueling stations. This station was the second to last one we would encounter before we finally reached our new home.

As we approached the marked area, we noticed a figure nearby. The closer we got, the clearer it became what it was; from afar, it resembled some sort of animal, maybe a coyote or a dog. Sure enough, when we got up close, we discovered it was indeed a dog. It had begun to dig at the spot. I carefully went up to him alone. I called out, "Here boy," and he quickly turned to me and came my way.

It was a Belgian Malinois dog. He had a color and a tag attached to him. When I checked his tag, it only displayed his name: "Justice." He was such a sweet dog, not aggressive at all: at least not with us. He appeared to be very hungry. We chose to keep digging in the spot where Justice had been digging, and we uncovered Jed's hidden treasure! More food and treats, enough for everyone, including Justice.

That turned out to be a great day; not only did we get back on track and locate Jed's refueling spot, but we also ended up with a dog. I really enjoy it when everything falls into place. Aside from being a bit underweight—who isn't these days?—Justice seemed quite healthy. We looked around to ensure his owner wasn't nearby. Then I asked the guys, "Should we keep him?"

Everyone replied in unison, "Absolutely! For sure! Not only will he add to our security team, but he will also provide great company and be a wonderful companion during chilly nights." It felt like the dog was genuinely happy to see us and couldn't stop expressing his gratitude. Justice was a fantastic addition to our team. He truly was a great dog!

chapter five

TARGETED

"Then you will be handed over to be persecuted and put to death, and you will be hated by all nations because of me."

MATTHEW 24:9

The animosity directed toward Christians was truly appalling! Jed also cautioned us about this, stating that it would be a level of hatred the world has never seen before. He reminded us of the Scripture that tells us we are hated because they first hated Jesus. He uplifted our spirits by reminding us that nothing can compare to His love for us, and we must keep in mind that our present struggles pale in comparison to the glory we will experience in heaven when we are with Him!

The two witnesses, along with the multitude of Jews who had been spreading the good news, left a profound impact on those who were still lacking the mark. As a result, a large number of people committed their lives to the Lord. Among them were Josh and Mary, who were accompanying us on our journey.

Cohen sensed a looming threat from the two witnesses that had emerged, particularly because they showcased their divine authority by consistently declaring God's judgment on those who were marked and were directly countering Cohen and his misleading claims of peace and safety.

In addition, these two witnesses not only stopped all forms of rain, leading rapidly to a drought, but they also commanded the water in rivers and oceans to transform into blood. Cohen not only persisted in his battle against the unmarked but also escalated his offensive.

The OWFP developed and incorporated cutting-edge technology into their drones. These state-of-the-art drones had the capability to scan individuals from several miles away, accurately identifying whether they were marked or unmarked. Once identified, if the individual was not marked, the drones emitted a ray that immobilized you until they reached your location. This advancement significantly heightened the pressure on us. As a result, hiding became an even greater challenge than before.

Moreover, the smart chips implanted in the designated individuals had evolved to such an extent that they could now reverse their aging process and enhance their strength and capabilities. It appeared that those who were marked were growing more powerful while we were becoming increasingly vulnerable. This situation only intensified the strain on our already diminished condition.

Cohen made sweeping promises to all who chose to accept the mark. He guaranteed them not only good health but also a sense of security, lasting peace, and the attainment of wealth and success. If our eyes had not been opened to the true implications behind these promises, it is highly likely that we would have been swept up in the frenzy, eager to acquire the mark as swiftly as we could.

Regardless of the challenges we faced, we grasped the reality of our situation and felt no desire to change any aspect of it. We had come to the profound understanding that our time in this world was temporary, whereas the essence of eternity endures forever.

FIELD OF DECISIONS

Cohen remained steadfast in his relentless campaign against the unmarked individuals, refusing to back down despite the challenges he faced. We discovered that he had built an enormous facility and adjacent to it a wide-open field that was exclusively filled with countless rows of guillotines, each one a grim reminder of the fate that awaited those who fell into his hands.

This ominous site was referred to as the Field of Decisions (FOD), a chilling name that underscored the gravity of the choices made there. It was within this harrowing location that the unmarked were taken after being apprehended, transported in large groups by bus, their fates sealed as they arrived at that dreadful destination.

As they positioned the head of the unmarked individual through these guillotines, they would pose a single question: Are you prepared to accept the mark to escape this punishment? If you answered affirmatively, they would follow up with another inquiry before setting you free: When you accept this mark, are you ready to renounce Jesus Christ as your Savior? For those who agreed and took the mark, that was the conclusion of the matter; they were marked, dealt with, and released.

In contrast, those who refused the mark faced execution. Furthermore, for those who denied the mark while traveling with loved ones, they would inflict torture on their loved ones right before their eyes until they renounced Jesus as their Savior, after which they would execute them, but not before subjecting them to torture as well.

Everyone did their best to keep going on the journey, even though we were aware of the terrible news. Mary and Josh were the ones who informed us about this situation. They also mentioned that it was impossible to buy food or anything else. A few of their friends had attempted to purchase some groceries from a corner store using a couple of gold coins, but the owner not only refused to sell food to them but also quickly reported them to the OWFP.

Josh went on, "It's incredible how quickly the OWFP reacted, almost as if they had been waiting just outside the store. Unfortunately, our friends were taken. That was the last time we saw them. With nothing to eat, we became so desperate that those in hiding would fight to the death over a filthy rat.

"I would have given anything to turn back time," Josh said. "Both of my parents were devoted Christians, and I should have known better. They always encouraged me to join them for church, but I found it dull; I believed religion was only for the older folks. My parents always begged Mary and me to come along.

"We got married when we were quite young; I met Mary during my college years. I had just begun my career when everything changed. We were enjoying our dream life until the disappearances occurred. I had recently been employed by a highly successful firm, receiving a sign-up bonus that was nearly double my first-year salary.

"Unfortunately, we lost everything shortly after that incident. Our senior partner, a dedicated Christian man, also vanished. Consequently, the firm started to unravel; and to make matters worse, the building that housed our office collapsed due to one of the initial tremors.

"If only I could go back and make everything right with God instead of focusing on my career, Mary and I wouldn't be in this predicament."

Mary then interjected, "No, Josh! It's not your fault; I had my own choices to make. I also knew better! My grandmother was a strong devoted woman of God, who would always warn us in love. I didn't listen!

"Just like you, Josh, I used to think I had all the time in the world to dedicate my life to Christ. I believed that focusing on my studies and our marriage was what mattered most. I always thought that only the truly wicked would be left behind. Since I attended church my entire life and both my parents and grandparents were saved, I assumed I was fine too.

"Now I realize it was never about being good or bad; we are all flawed. It's the sin within us that makes us imperfect, which is why we needed to establish a personal relationship with Jesus, as He is our only genuine Savior.

"So, Josh, it's not just on you; we all share the blame. Each of us had our own decisions to make."

Jasmine chimed in, saying, "Exactly, Mary: we are solely responsible for the outcomes in our lives. Our buddy Jed, the one who wrote this journal and left it for us, tried to warn us repeatedly, but we ignored him.

"We first met Jedidiah in our freshman year of high school. Richard, David, Alli, Regi, and I were the closest of friends, totally inseparable."

Mary asked, "Who's Regi?"

Jasmine replied, "She was a really good friend of ours who also vanished, along with Jed and his fiancée, Grace.

"I didn't have a church upbringing or anyone in my family to teach me about God, but that's not a good excuse because God still sent someone my way. He sent Jed, and now

I realize that, but I was really set in my own ways. Honestly, before Jed, I didn't even think God existed. Like many folks, I just thought you should live your best life here, make the most of it, and when you die, that's the end, game over.

"Jed never gave up on us; he never pressured anyone, but man, he was very persistent about inviting us. He had this unique way of making you feel loved, the good kind of love, you know? He asked us to join him for his Bible study group several times, but each time I turned him down. You should have seen the hurt in his eyes.

"I felt disappointed in myself as well, but I just couldn't bring myself to go or even hear what he had to say. As a friend, I truly loved him! He meant a lot to us and still does. Without him, we wouldn't have a plan right now. I probably would have ended up taking the mark like everyone else."

THE GATHERINGS

The sun had been becoming increasingly hot. Our skin began to blister in various exposed spots. We did our utmost to shield ourselves, yet we still got burned. Because of the intense heat, we made the decision to rest during the day and walk at night. This was very risky, but given the situation, it seemed like we had no other option.

Both Jasmine and I took the first watch, while the others attempted to catch some sleep. It wasn't easy at all; it felt like we were more exhausted than ever, but we understood deep down that we had to keep going no matter what. We were so close, yet still so far away.

After nearly a week of daytime sleeping and nighttime walking, we stumbled upon an old warehouse. It appeared to have been deserted for some time, even prior to the disappearances. We thought it would be an ideal place to take refuge during the day and escape the sun.

We thoroughly inspected the whole area, just like we always do. We ensured there were no traps of any kind or any cameras or surveillance systems. David and Alli chose to take the first watch this morning. We were exhausted; all of us were really worn out.

I'm not quite sure where we went wrong or how it occurred, but we had been asleep for a few hours, and even David and Alli had dozed off. Suddenly, we were jolted awake by someone using a bullhorn. It was the OWFP!

The soldier holding the bullhorn instructed us to exit the premises with our hands raised above our heads, promising that no one would be injured in the process. He explained that they had been monitoring our activities for several days, and this was the culmination of their efforts to finally apprehend us.

Upon arriving at the warehouse, I recalled noticing a large drainage system at the back. I couldn't quite explain why, but it seemed spacious enough for all of us to fit inside. At that moment, Mary stood up and reassured us, saying, "Don't worry, everyone. I've got this covered."

Without hesitating for even a second, Mary made the bold decision to step outside, raising her arms high above her head. She shouted, "Don't shoot, I'm unarmed! Here I am, take me! I'm all alone!"

In a frantic attempt to reach her, Josh sprinted after her. We tried our best to restrain him, but he was resolute in his determination not to leave his wife alone. The OWFP quickly apprehended them and inquired about the whereabouts of the others. Mary and Josh maintained that they were by themselves. What Mary and Josh did provided us with sufficient time to flee through the drainage system. Even Justice managed to escape with us.

Our hearts were broken in pieces; we had just experienced the devastating loss of two dear friends. In that moment of grief, we made a solemn vow not to forsake them. We were resolute in our commitment to do everything in our power to try and rescue them.

The FOD was relatively close, requiring at most a three-day walk. We easily picked up the tracks of the OWFP's vehicle. During our journey, we devised a plan to attempt to rescue our friends.

When we arrived at the FOD, it was even more shocking than we had thought. From our vantage point, we could observe the entire operation unfold. The unmarked individuals were quickly taken to an outdoor holding area where they were rounded up and processed like livestock. After that, they were stripped of all their belongings and handed an orange jumpsuit to wear. It didn't matter if they were male, female, young, or old; everyone was kept in the same holding area and treated the same.

This bought us some time, since our friends had not yet been taken to the decision area. However, considering how quickly the OWFP was moving forward, it was just a matter of time before they would get to our friends.

David was all set with his rifle; he was prepared to take anyone out at a moment's notice. We believed our plan was simple: first, we would create a distraction; and as soon as the OWFP reacted to it, our next step would be to move in, eliminate whoever we needed to, and save our friends.

What transpired next took us by surprise. Before we could realize it, our friend Josh was being guided toward one of the guillotines. As his head was positioned in the opening, our hearts dropped. Mary let out a desperate cry, and it felt like time had frozen.

I realized it was a now-or-never moment, so I signaled Jasmine. The moment I did, she detonated a vehicle that was stationed just outside the compound. Several of the OWFP rushed to investigate the site of the explosion, but their commander quickly issued the command to execute those in place. With the press of a single button, all the guillotines were set into motion.

Our dear friend Josh was gone! Mary found herself in shock; amid the chaos, she managed to disarm one of the OWFP guards. She began firing at all the guards surrounding her. Unfortunately, a guard stationed high in a guard shack swiftly ended Mary's life.

RESILIENCE

When we finally reached our rally point, we ensured that everyone was all right. Jeremiah and Sarah were waiting for us there. They inquired if everything was fine, having heard the explosion they felt concerned.

They asked about Josh and Mary. As soon as they saw our expressions, they instinctively understood that they hadn't survived. We had to push forward, even in the face of our loss; we had come too far to be defeated now.

Jeremiah inquired about our next step. I replied, "Let's keep moving forward. We will miss Josh and Mary, and we will reunite with them eventually, but if we don't speed up now, we might end up seeing them sooner than we anticipated."

It was becoming increasingly difficult; the nights appeared to stretch endlessly. The sole source of solace we found was in reading God's Word during our journey. Additionally, Jed's notcs provided us with valuable support and something to look forward to.

We discovered a large oak tree along the way, and it appeared to be an ideal spot to take a break for the day. Everyone settled into their chosen spots and quickly fell asleep. I was the first to take the watch, and while I was on guard, I kept hearing a familiar sound coming from a short distance away. I woke David and requested that he take over the watch while I went to investigate the surroundings.

I recognized that sound; it was clearly coming from a beeyard. My knowledge of beekeeping comes from my childhood memories with my grandfather, who was really into beekeeping. He passed down a lot of his wisdom about bees to me, sharing important lessons and insights before he left us.

This was truly a gift from God. I had never approached a bee box without the right gear before, but given the situation, a few stings wouldn't be the end of the world. When I opened the box and reached for the frame, it surprisingly went smoother than I expected, almost as if the bees were eager to share their honey without any trouble.

In a rush, I woke up the guys, since we hadn't eaten in ages and this was just what we needed. The girls were super surprised, asking, "What is it?" Honey! Just pure honey and honeycomb. Alli wondered if it was edible, and when I said yes, everyone pretty much attacked me for some. Even Justice got in on it, and he loved it! I made sure to tell everyone that there was more than enough to share and that there was more where that came from.

This got us ready to continue our journey. We kept moving along the trail next to the river, fueled by the hope of reaching Jed's family home. A lot had happened over the past two years, but we knew even more was coming our way. The Scriptures suggested we were nearing the midpoint of the tribulation, and we could feel that major events were about to unfold.

Just when we thought everything was getting better, out of nowhere a strong gust of wind hit us, which felt nice, but what came next was totally surprising. The wind was so fierce that we quickly took shelter under a nearby tree. Just as we got under the tree, huge chunks of hail began to fall from the sky. These weren't your average hailstones; they were as big as a truck. Even though we had faced a lot, this was one of the scariest experiences we had to go through. Thank goodness, none of us got hurt.

Feeling utterly drained and terrified, we decided it was best to take a break that day. As we turned on the radio, we were met with the alarming news that thousands of people had sustained injuries from the hailstorm that had ravaged the area. The level of destruction and chaos caused by that storm was unprecedented, impacting both the marked and unmarked.

Cohen spoke to the worldwide audience with a serious declaration: Only the unmarked had suffered injuries and fatalities due to the unyielding hail. He went on to emphasize that this further demonstrated the necessity of addressing and eliminating the unmarked at any cost.

THE FAITHFUL

A few days after the hailstorm, we were thrilled to find that according to Jed's map, we were nearly at his last refueling station. This not only signified that we would be able to eat, it also meant we were closer than ever to finally returning home.

While we were enjoying our meal, a report came in that the Overseer had some great news for everyone. Whatever that news was, we understood that good news for them usually meant bad news for us. Then the next announcement was: "We got them—we finally caught those two troublemaking false messengers. They had aimed to topple our cherished Cohen, but fate finally intervened, and they got what was coming to them.

"Furthermore, we have captured a significant amount of the unmarked. To commemorate this, we will showcase the deceased bodies of the two individuals in the public plaza in front of the OWGO headquarters for everyone to witness. Cohen has proclaimed today a day of triumph and has announced this entire week will be a period of festivity."

Our hearts sank when we learned about the tragic event that had just occurred. What does this mean? What does it signify for us Christians who are still around? Just when it seemed like we were on the brink of despair, Jasmine brought up Jed's note: "Hey everyone, DON'T BE SAD! When you hear or see that the two witnesses are dead, don't be scared! That just means our God is getting ready to show His power to this wicked and corrupt generation. They're about to find out who the one true God is. THEY ARE ALIVE!!!"

Was it possible? Did that really mean that the two witnesses were still alive? But their bodies were right there in the plaza, showcasing Cohen's triumph. "We have to trust, believe, and be patient," Jasmine said. "We need to stay faithful and keep moving forward, regardless of what we witness happening around us. God is bigger than anything Cohen or this world can throw at us.

"The sacrifices made by our Lord Jesus Christ and those who came before us should inspire us to live a life that honors Him and others. Take Mary, for instance; her actions weren't driven by her own strength, but rather by her deep love for God and for us. This kind of love isn't something you find in the world or in a mark. It's a sacrificial love that comes solely from God.

"I realize now that this is what motivated Jed all those years to warn us; and not just that, but he even went out of his way to leave us this journal along with everything else. This is the same kind of love that inspired Jed's grandpa to construct, equip, and leave us the bunker. Seriously, who else would do something like that for total strangers?

"As we explore the Bible together, we can clearly see that the theme of love radiates throughout its verses. It is essential for us to come together and share the blessings and insights we have received with each other. Therefore, let us remember Jed's encouraging notes: There is no need to fear, for God is always present with us!"

After three days of gift exchanges in celebration of the death of the two witnesses, something amazing happened. This important event was aired on TV and broadcast over the radio, reaching audiences all around the globe.

Just when Cohen and all the marked individuals believed they had triumphed, lo and behold, the two witnesses rose again before everyone. They came to life and stood up; and as if that weren't astonishing enough, they ascended into the clouds right before the eyes of all. The entire world was observing, and everyone was in disbelief at what they had just witnessed.

Across the globe, individuals lamented what had just occurred, while Cohen found himself at a loss to articulate the events that had just unfolded. There was nothing within his power to reverse the reality they had just experienced. Now, more than at any other time, people began to scrutinize the falsehoods they had been fed. They started proclaiming that the two witnesses were indeed the genuine prophets of the one true God.

chapter six

IT WILL GET WORSE

"I have told you these things so that in Me you may have peace. In the world you will have tribulation. But take courage; I have overcome the world!"

JOHN 16:33

Cohen understood that his time was limited; he had only a brief period to achieve what he had long desired. Following the death and resurrection of the two witnesses, many turned against the OWGO. Numerous individuals questioned Cohen's true nature, aware that he was not the one true God. Despite his declaration of divinity in the Jewish temple, they remained skeptical. Many recalled the words spoken by the two witnesses, including several who had received the mark of the beast. They came to the realization of their actions, understanding that they had surrendered their lives to the anti-Christ, the embodiment of Satan, but it was already too late.

One evening while walking, we suddenly felt a tremendous jolt beneath our feet, as if another earthquake was approaching. The earth trembled under us, and we were powerless to react; however, to our astonishment, the shaking was brief. What had just happened felt unusual. This was not your typical earthquake.

As we listened to the radio, breaking news reported that a colossal asteroid, referred to as Wormwood, had collided with the West Coast and the surrounding ocean. This catastrophic event led to the tragic loss of millions of lives. In the days that followed, the situation worsened as hundreds more succumbed to the effects of drinking water that had been tainted by the aftermath of the impact.

The event was truly devastating, leaving us with a profound sense of sorrow. As we reflected on the tough situation, a heavy feeling of despair enveloped us. In that moment, we found ourselves praying with an intensity we had never experienced before, not only for our own safety but also for our fellow Christian brothers and sisters. We were acutely aware that many of them were also hiding and feeling hopeless. Our hearts connected with them in solidarity.

It had been ages since we'd found a good spot to relax. We frequently speculated about what we would discover when we eventually reached Jed's family farm. We prayed and wished that it hadn't been destroyed or taken over by others. We only had a short distance left to travel. Everyone sensed that perhaps, just maybe, God was planning to use us out here one last time.

NOWHERE TO HIDE

We stumbled upon a ranger station that had been partly ruined by the earthquakes, but it provided decent shade from the sun. Inside, we discovered some comfortable cots. We definitely needed this break. David and Alli drew straws for watch duty first. While we were catching some z's, David suddenly woke us up in a panic, looking terrified. I asked him what was happening, and all he and Alli could do was gesture toward the window.

Without any warning, a thick darkness swept over the area, just like nightfall. Almost immediately, a loud, overwhelming buzzing sound filled the air, as if a massive swarm of bees were drawing near. My curiosity got the better of me, and I leaned closer to the window. What I saw completely blew my mind. Thousands of enormous creatures were soaring through the sky, each one as large as a horse and bearing a striking resemblance to flying scorpions.

We couldn't believe what was happening. All we could do was hold each other tight and pray—and boy, did we pray! A couple of those creatures stopped to peek through the window, but as soon as they touched down, they quickly took off. Once again, we relied on our trusty book, Jed's journal; and sure enough, this incident was recorded there. He had included the entry in his footnotes. He mentioned that seven judgments from God were set to occur soon after the disappearances. This particular judgment was outlined in the book of Revelation, chapter 9.

It was wild to see all of this unfold right in front of us. We started to wonder if anyone else was going through the same thing, so we switched on the radio to get the scoop. News was pouring in from everywhere, saying these creatures were going after anyone who had the mark. It felt like they had just one goal, and that was to target the marked.

Many people suffered painful stings from these creatures, and reports indicated that the agony was so intense that numerous individuals found themselves wishing for death as a release from their suffering, yet they were unable to escape it. Despite the excruciating pain they endured, which led them to curse and express their anger toward God, they still held no regrets about their decision to take the mark. The torment they experienced was overwhelming, but their commitment to their choice remained steadfast.

We carried on with our journey until Justice suddenly began barking loudly, almost as if trying to alert us that someone or something was lurking ahead on the path. David chose to investigate while we concealed ourselves among the nearby brush.

David yelled urgently, "Richard, get the med-kit!" Without hesitation, I responded, and Justice joined us as well. Upon reaching the scene, I was struck by the sight of two OWFP soldiers sprawling on the ground next to their vehicle, writhing in agony. They were clearly suffering from the effects of the stings inflicted by those creatures we had faced just a few nights earlier.

The girls hung back with Jeremiah and Sarah, while David and I did our best to assist the soldiers. Their injuries were really deep and serious, almost like they had been pierced by some kind of spear. They had several wounds all over their bodies. We did everything we could to help them, but no matter what we tried, they were in intense pain.

Out of the blue, a third soldier appeared, aiming his gun at us. Before we had a chance to respond, Justice leaped right at the soldier and bit his gun hand, making him drop his weapon. David got up and questioned the soldier: "What's wrong with you, man? Don't you realize that we are here to help you and your friends? What were you thinking?"

The soldier responded firmly, stating, "We have been given strict orders to detain anyone who lacks the mark, and it appears that all of you are unmarked." He continued: "If we do not address this situation swiftly, we will encounter even more severe repercussions."

I then turned to the soldier and pleaded, "Can't you understand that we are merely just trying to help?"

David secured the soldiers by placing their own handcuffs on them while we managed the situation. Once we had finished dealing with them, we considered the possibility of taking their vehicle. However, we quickly realized that neither the vehicle nor their weapons were operational for us. It became clear that these items were only functional for individuals who bore the mark.

Rather than take a more direct approach, we decided to

deflate all the tires of their vehicle, disable their communication equipment, and take their weapons. Our plan was to transport the weapons to a remote location, ensuring they were disposed of far from the soldiers' reach.

Now that they knew we were here, we needed to take a different path than the one we had been following. We needed to ensure that we covered our tracks more effectively, but we also couldn't proceed on our journey in a straight line. We needed to throw the soldiers off by heading in the opposite direction, then looping back around further ahead. This would prolong our journey and make it more challenging, but if we wanted to make it through this, we had no other option.

THE BETRAYAL

Cohen realized he was losing support among his followers; everything that had happened and was happening was undermining his hold on the world. He understood the urgency to act swiftly before he lost even more of his believers. This was particularly crucial, as many of the Jews had escaped to the mountains immediately after he proclaimed himself to be God in their temple.

A major announcement was scheduled to be broadcast worldwide, reaching viewers all over the globe. This broadcast was mandatory, which meant that anyone who had the mark was required to watch it, with no possibility of opting out.

The Overseer was the first to address the audience, expressing his gratitude to everyone present and those tuning into the broadcast. He went on to criticize the true God and condemn the unmarked. He stated that even though the unmarked had previously escaped and false messengers had disseminated their falsehoods, this did not alter the fact of who the one and only God truly was: our cherished Cohen.

As the audience listened intently, the Overseer continued: "Cohen is truly our one and only God, deserving of our worship. To emphasize this, I present to you, his heir." Suddenly, a massive, monstrous figure that bore a striking resemblance to Cohen emerged. This creature was mesmerizing, but not in a positive sense. An unsettling silence followed as the being made its entrance.

Cohen then began his speech by addressing the crowd, saying, "My dear children, we have faced many challenges together, and while we have endured some difficult times, those days are behind us. From this moment forward, I will bless you as you honor my heir, and I will shower you with blessings. The more you worship me, the more I will look after you. All I ask in return is that you stay devoted to me and worship your one true God!"

The Overseer then declared, "To guarantee that everyone abides by this, we have enacted this as a formal law. If you decide to ignore this law, you will be subject to immediate execution. When the alarm sounds, it is your duty to bow down and worship your God!"

Shortly after the Overseer concluded his speech, the alarm sounded. Many of the marked individuals bowed down and began to worship the beast. However, a few chose not to comply, and what happened next was quite bizarre: A laser beam shot out from the giant and instantly killed those who refused to worship Cohen.

This fate also befell individuals in other parts of the world. Upon hearing the alarm, they were compelled to abandon their activities and worship the beast on the spot or face dire consequences. In a strange twist, if they decided to ignore the alarm and not worship the beast, their chip would self-destruct, leading to their immediate demise.

The days we went through were packed with huge challenges, which just piled on the chaos around us. We were in a never-ending fight, dealing with not just outside troubles but also our own inner battles. In the middle of all this chaos, Jesus stood out as our true source of peace, leading us through the rough times.

TEMPORARY REFUGE

The intensity of the situation had escalated significantly; the new entity brought forth by the Overseer was not merely capable of observing the marked individuals and monitoring their every move but also possessed the remarkable ability to detect those who were unmarked and chase after them with unwavering determination.

We quickly realized that finding shelter was imperative, and we understood the necessity of hiding ourselves from potential threats. Our new home was within reach, yet our recent encounter with the OWFP soldiers forced us to take a longer, more indirect route, which would certainly delay our progress.

Nearby, there were several hills that piqued our interest, and we felt it would be worthwhile exploring them. We hoped to find some form of shelter to take refuge in for the time being. As we made our way closer, we decided to take a leisurely walk around the perimeter of the hills first.

Justice chose to sprint ahead of us, and halfway through, he took off like a rocket. We shouted for him to come back, but he kept running forward. If it weren't for Justice, we would have totally missed it. There was an opening on the side of the hill, but it was hidden from view. It was situated on the inner side of a fold in the hill, perfectly camouflaged from outsiders.

David and I thought it would be smart to check out the area ourselves before the rest of the team went in, just to make sure everything was safe. When we stepped into the cave, we saw that there were no signs of anyone having been there for quite a while. We pressed on deeper into the cave, excited to discover what was hidden inside.

We entered what looked like a room chiseled out of the rock, and when I shone my light around, I spotted the creepiest thing just sitting on the floor. It totally freaked us out—it was a skeleton. You could tell it had been there for ages, even before the disappearances happened. There was another area that connected to this one, and inside, we discovered all sorts of handmade furniture.

As we kept digging, we found more items and personal belongings, indicating that this person had been living here for quite a while. After we cleared away the debris and mess, we thought it would be a good idea to call in the rest of our team for a deeper look. To our surprise, we realized that this individual seemed to have been a veteran who had chosen to live off-grid on their own.

One of the most surprising discoveries we made was an ice box or container that had been ingeniously integrated into the floor itself. This hidden compartment was packed with a variety of food items stored in jars and cans, and to our astonishment, a significant portion of it was still safe to eat. Additionally, we stumbled upon a fascinating water system that this individual had constructed, utilizing the natural rock formations around them to create an effective means of water collection and distribution.

In a remarkable display of creativity, he had managed to channel the water from a nearby creek right into his house. After looking into it more, we discovered that he didn't just direct the water into his home; he also had cleverly built a natural filtration system that cleaned the water before it entered his living area. This smart arrangement made sure the water was safe and clean for use, highlighting his ingenuity.

We were completely speechless, and it dawned on us once more that this was undoubtedly a divine blessing! This location was perfect for us to stay for a while before making our way to Jed's house.

Another amazing feature we found in the cave was a clever natural lighting setup. The person had skillfully arranged a bunch of mirrors to bounce sunlight from the entrance, resulting in a surprisingly efficient lighting system. It was really interesting to observe how he had linked these mirrors to a lever, making it easy to tweak the angle of the light. Plus, while we were exploring, we found some candles, which helped for lighting at night.

That night we had a deep and restful sleep, something we hadn't had in what felt like forever; it was like we had been asleep for days. When we finally woke up, we felt totally refreshed and ready to tackle whatever challenges were coming our way.

Still, we decided to play it safe and wait a few weeks before making any moves, wanting to see how things would unfold in the outside world. We were especially cautious about the possible threats from the OWFP and the huge creature hanging around, and we didn't want to take any unnecessary chances.

NEW STRENGTH

Time flew by fast while we were in the cave. We stumbled upon a journal left by the last person who had stayed there. Reading it really made the hours fly by. As we read through it, we learned that the man's name was Bill and that he had spent his entire life in the military. He wrote about being part of various conflicts and how he felt he couldn't fit into society anymore, so he chose to live out there in the wild.

Bill, who remained single, had had no living relatives to refer to as family. He often wrote about his companionship with his dog, Trigger. Despite our extensive search efforts, we were unable to find Trigger. It is our belief that when Bill passed away, Trigger may have roamed away.

The more we read, the heavier our hearts felt. Bill also shared that he had battled a form of cancer through the end of his lifetime and was aware that his time was limited. He expressed gratitude for his deceased Brother Tony, a man of faith who had guided him to the Lord.

Our new friend Bill was also a believer in Christ! This gave us hope that we will have the opportunity to reunite with him in the future. When that day comes, we can take the time to express our heartfelt gratitude for what he did for us. Without realizing it, he saved our lives by providing temporary refuge for us.

Because Bill had saved our lives and was truly a blessing from the Lord, we felt it was only right to give him a burial. Thanks to his home, we could have stayed there indefinitely if necessary, but deep down we understood that our true mission was to reach Jed's place.

For a long time, there was something we all wanted to do but never found the chance to make it happen. With Bill's creek nearby, we figured it was the ideal moment to get baptized. Most of the group nominated me to take the lead on this, and I happily agreed.

One by one, all my friends got baptized in the name of our Lord and Savior, Jesus Christ. What an exhilarating moment it was! In that instant, we all sensed His presence like never before—it felt like we had been given a new strength from above! When it was my turn, David happily volunteered to baptize me.

We all came together in a heartfelt embrace, shedding tears that flowed like never before. This was not a cry of sorrow, but rather an expression of unadulterated joy! A resounding "Hallelujah, praise God!" burst forth from my lips! To our surprise, even Jeremiah and Sarah joined in and requested to get baptized. What amazed us even more was that Justice stood right there in the middle of our celebration, sharing the moment with us.

What an unforgettable day it was! We will always hold it dear in our hearts. Following that incredible experience, we decided to celebrate by preparing a special meal with the limited ingredients we had on hand. It felt like we were indulging in a five-course feast, because at that moment, nothing could dampen our spirits.

THE LAST STRETCH

For a brief period, the chaos outside seemed to subside, bringing a sense of temporary peace. We could have remained in the cave a little longer, enjoying the tranquility; but one evening, just as we were getting ready to settle in for the night, we suddenly felt the earth begin to shake beneath us.

We instinctively understood what it was. Recognizing that it wasn't safe indoors, we quickly gathered our gear and headed outside. Our equipment was always prepared for action, a lesson we had learned from David and Jasmine's military training. They taught us from the start that our gear should always be ready, regardless of the situation.

Good thing we came out when we did—as soon as the last of us made our way out, the entrance to the cave collapsed. Although we would definitely miss that spot, we understood that our time here was over.

At that point, we quickened our steps and kept moving ahead. We aimed to retrace our route to the place where we had run into the soldiers before. Even though it was likely they had already left, we remained focused on being careful and staying alert as we went along.

As soon as we reached the location where we had the encounter with the soldiers, we had just one day's travel left before finally reaching the farm. The thrill and anticipation we experienced about getting to our destination were nearly palpable, creating an atmosphere filled with urgency and hope.

On our way toward Jed's farm, we noticed a striking change in the scenery around us. The things we recognized started to disappear, making it harder to tell if we were on the right path. This doubt grew stronger since we decided to travel at night to escape the sweltering heat of the sun.

We kept going on our journey, holding on to our faith in God, knowing that our own efforts wouldn't be enough. It was His divine support that had brought us that far, and we truly believed that only by following His guidance would we reach our final destination.

On our final stretch, we encountered two girls on the path, clearly distressed and in tears. Aware that this could be a possible trap, we proceeded carefully and slowly closed the gap between us and the girls.

Justice carried out the first inspection, hurrying over to them and took a good sniff. We knew that all was well when he started to lick their faces. The girls began giggling when he did that. Justice had a way of making people feel better in the midst of pain.

When we inquired about their well-being, the first thing we noticed was that they were twins. The next thing we looked for was whether they were marked or unmarked. We discovered that they were, in fact, unmarked. One of the girls mentioned that they were not doing well. She explained that their father had been injured while attempting to rescue them from a tree that had fallen during the earthquake.

We asked whether their mother or anyone else was with them. They mentioned that their mom was among those who disappeared and that they had been living with their dad on their farm. However, they had run out of food, which is why they were searching for some when the tremor happened.

We asked the girls—Zoe and Jubilee—if they would like to come with us on our trip. They were interested in where we were going and wanted to learn more. We shared the details of our journey with them, and they were eager to join us. Even though they missed their father, they understood that they couldn't stay alone during these tough times.

They shared that they had been praying for help and felt that they might perish out there alone. Unsure of what to do next, they recalled their mother's advice: "Daughters, if you ever find yourselves in danger and see no way out, the wisest thing to do is pray. He will listen when you speak sincerely from your heart."

chapter seven

THE ARRIVAL

The Lord says, "I will guide you along the best pathway for your life. I will advise you and watch over you."

PSALM 32:8

The moment we arrived we felt surreal: it was hard to believe we had reached our destination. Jed's family farm, at last! Every struggle, every conflict, and all the hardships we faced were all worth it! The happiness we felt was unlike anything we had encountered throughout our journey. What was supposed to be just a few days of walking had ended up taking years. We weren't complaining, though; it was astonishing what we had just gone through. Getting there was certainly not solely due to our own strength.

I found it hard to believe what we had just gone through. We had faced an immense number of challenges, and there had been countless instances when I doubted our ability to survive; this ordeal truly opened my eyes to my actual state of being. Prior to the disappearances, I can honestly say that I often took life for granted. Looking back now, I realize that as a community, we were exceedingly spoiled.

I began to realize that we had been given everything on a silver platter and that as a society, we had settled into a state of complacency. Advancements in technology had made it possible for us to acquire anything we want with just a simple tap of our fingers. Instead of appreciating the things we already had, we had developed a sense of entitlement, constantly craving for processes to be more automated and faster. This shift in mindset had led us to overlook the value of hard work and the satisfaction that came from earning what we desired.

This situation created a shared mindset in society that made us think we didn't need God anymore. We began to see ourselves as fully independent people. But the reality was that our dependence on technology had grown significantly, to the point where it had basically taken on the role of God in our everyday lives.

I am truly grateful to God for His endless mercy that He always shows us. Even when we stray from the path He has set for us, He kindly motivates friends and family, like Jed, to stay committed to connecting with us and spreading the gospel message. Thanks to Jed's steadfast dedication and his willingness to follow God's call, we have felt God's constant support and direction in our lives.

Following Jed's advice from his journal, we made our way into the property through the back entrance. David and I agreed that it would be best to systematically inspect the area, focusing on one building at a time. We decided to start with the old barn, which looked as though it had been left alone for many years, its weathered exterior telling stories of neglect and time.

The next area we cleared was the newer barn, which seemed to be empty as well. After that we headed to the house, entering through the back and thoroughly clearing each room one at a time.

In the last bedroom, we heard a strange noise, which led us to enter together. While David checked the right side, I went to the left; as we stepped in, I saw something move in the closet. When I got closer for a better look, I found a family of raccoons that had been living there for a considerable time.

David and I burst into laughter when we discovered that it was just a family of raccoons that had frightened us so badly. Wow, were we relieved it was only raccoons! Everything could have turned out quite differently if it had been someone else.

As soon as we walked into the kitchen, we couldn't help but notice Jed's grandparents' clothes left on the floor. These pieces were the only real proof that they were ever here, a harsh reminder of all the family and friends who had disappeared from our lives. Their left-behind clothing acted as a bittersweet emblem of the past, stirring up memories of what used to be.

OUR NEW HOME

Once we made sure that the whole farm was completely free of any dangers, we shifted our focus to the old barn. We were excited to delve into its insides and uncover any treasures or surprises it might contain, as it was set to be our new home.

Jed told us there was a trap door located right under his grandfather's worktable. But before we could go in, we had to find the key that was hidden behind the horseshoe on the wall. Just as Jed said, the key was exactly where he pointed it out. We felt a mix of excitement and fear all at once.

During our time in the open, we stumbled upon an important finding: It wasn't safe for everyone to go into a certain area at the same time. This led us to understand that our previous idea of breaking into smaller groups was definitely the smartest move. With this in mind, Jasmine and I decided to head in first while the others waited in a safe place.

When we reached the bottom of the stairs, we found another door. Above the door frame, there was a little sign that said "The Ark." We tried to open it, but it was locked. At that moment, Jasmine recalled that the key was hidden under the last stair. And sure enough, it was right where we were told it would be.

At long last, the moment we had eagerly anticipated had finally come. As we swung open the door, what lay before us was nothing short of astonishing. The entryway greeted us with a modest foyer, leading into a kitchen area that featured a small table neatly positioned along the side. Beyond that, we were met with two rows of four bunk beds on either side, all meticulously organized and arranged.

As we kept exploring, we realized there was even more

to uncover. We stumbled upon a second chamber, and as we stepped inside, we felt a noticeable drop in temperature. There were countless large containers packed with all sorts of food; enough to sustain an army for years on end. We also came across a water fountain area, complete with some kind of water filtration system. It was incredible. That must have taken ages to put together.

In addition to the two larger chambers, there was a compact third chamber that contained a variety of essential survival equipment. This included all kinds of tools, an assortment of weapons for protection, and ammunition to accompany them. Furthermore, the chamber was stocked with several articles of clothing suitable for both men and women, ensuring that anyone who found themselves in need would have access to the necessary gear.

We brought the rest of the team inside. We made sure that both the upper and lower doors were securely closed, just like Jed suggested. The crew was amazed; they couldn't believe what they were seeing. They were surprised by how much space there was for eight people, plus our dog, and it ended up being surprisingly cozy.

We had just started to get comfortable when Jasmine stumbled upon a secret door hidden behind the last room. Our curiosity got the better of us, and when we opened the door, we were amazed to discover a series of tunnels that took us straight to the forest. It was an awesome escape route, a clever backup plan for any tricky situation we might face. Jed's grandpa really had thought of everything. To our surprise, this place even had a shower area, which made it even more appealing and useful.

After we finished our showers and got dressed, it struck us that it had been some time since we had the chance to make a warm, comforting meal. The idea of doing this felt particularly special to us, so we took a moment to stop and express our sincere gratitude to God for blessing us and enabling us to share this lovely experience together.

After we finished our dinner, we took some time to read the Bible. By the time we wrapped everything up, we were completely worn out. We must have slept for a full two days. When we finally woke up, we felt incredibly refreshed and energized. It was quite an unusual feeling; we weren't accustomed to being so clean and well-rested.

David and Alli enthusiastically volunteered to take charge of preparing breakfast for everyone that morning. Meanwhile, Jasmine and I decided to step outside and enjoy the fresh air. Jeremiah, Sarah, and the girls made the choice to remain indoors, opting for a little extra rest. We completely understood their decision; the last stretch of our journey had truly exhausted all of us.

Jasmine and I chose to take a walk around the property. We were amazed at how well everything had been preserved. The fires hadn't affected that whole area, and none of the other factors—like hail, earthquakes, or even the animals—appeared to have harmed the farm. The whole property felt like it was suspended in time.

We even spotted a couple of chickens still wandering about. The other animals appeared to have fled and got away. Aside from that, everything else still looked intact. This was genuinely a miracle from God.

I used to be skeptical about miracles, but since I've devoted my heart to Jesus, I have witnessed and experienced things that can only be described as miraculous. Praise God for His blessings.

ADJUSTING

Before long, everything started to come together. We adjusted to our new way of life quite smoothly. While we were sorting through the food supplies left by Jed's family, we discovered some heirloom seeds, which included a variety of vegetables, fruits, spices, and herbs. They had also left behind a book that provided us with all the knowledge we needed about seeds and gardening.

We made the choice to create a garden in a secluded spot far from the bunker, where it would be hidden from anyone passing by. Even if someone happened to discover it, they wouldn't recognize it as a natural garden because we disguised it with the surrounding landscape.

Gardening turned out to be a wonderfully calming and fulfilling activity. It was truly one of my most cherished tasks. Justice enjoyed accompanying me during my gardening sessions; he had a great time helping me dig the holes and was quite skilled at it.

Each person was assigned a distinct task or responsibility to complete throughout the day. In addition, the adults took turns handling security duties, allowing the rest to concentrate on their respective work. We had to stay alert, fully aware that numerous dangerous individuals were still in the area. Furthermore, we had to keep in mind that Cohen and the OWFP were still actively searching for the unmarked.

While Alli and the twins were tidying up our bunker, they stumbled across a box packed with board games, Bibles, and a mix of other books. This find was truly a lifesaver; when the girls eagerly told us about their discovery, we all felt a wave of excitement about the amazing treasure they had uncovered.

That night we played board games, and it was the most fun we'd had in ages. It was beginning to feel like a true home and we had all grown into a tight-knit family. We still thought about what was going on outside, concerned for our fellow brothers and sisters in Christ.

One of the things I loved most about our daily routine was starting each morning with a devotional, followed by prayer time and Bible study in the evenings. The twins were really into it too. We all learned a ton together, but I had to study a bit harder since I was chosen to be the group's minister.

Despite how rough things were in the outside world, I felt grateful for everything that happened. It might sound a bit nuts, but if none of those events had occurred, I wouldn't have met these amazing people, nor would I have come to know my Lord and Savior.

Alli created a schedule for everyone to stick to. It ran smoothly. She split it into four parts: work time, devotional time, play time, and personal time. During work time, David and I tackled some projects that helped the whole group. Some were successful, while others weren't; but overall, we were making strides as each day went by.

We had to ensure that everything we did left no trace or signs of our presence. The old barn was left just as we found it: cloaked in dust and spider webs. Spiders were our allies, providing the best natural camouflage, courtesy of God.

One evening, as we were preparing to go to bed, we heard some commotion coming from upstairs; it seemed someone had been shifting things around in the old barn. We had no idea who it was or how many people were involved. Everyone in the bunker, including Justice, stayed as quiet as possible.

Next, we heard vehicles moving around the property; we could distinctly hear them driving toward the house. We heard their laughter as they shattered the windows and walls of the home. What happened next took us by surprise. We could hear them driving away, but before they left, they tossed in a bottle filled with some kind of flammable liquid, which instantly set the home ablaze.

The house was entirely engulfed in flames, raging fiercely all night long, and we felt completely powerless to intervene. We understood that stepping in could put us in danger, and we weren't willing to take that chance. When morning finally arrived, David and I headed over to check out the damage. What we discovered was heartbreaking: Jed's family home had turned into nothing but ashes and debris. It was a tragic scene, and the loss hit us hard as we stood there, trying to process the devastation that had occurred.

We were uncertain about who had set the house on fire; we only had a suspicion that it was the OWFP. They were still searching for Christians and ensuring that no refuge remained for anyone.

THE MIDDLE

Following the fire, we became more cautious in all our actions. We understood that we still had a long way to go before things got better. We limited our outings, at least for some time, and when we did go out, it was only in groups of two or three.

According to the Bible and Jed's journal, we figured out that we had hit the halfway mark of the tribulation. What did this mean? It meant that things were about to get worse. At least for those outside.

It had been about six months since we first stepped into the Ark. Amazingly, it felt like we had just gotten there a few weeks back. During that time we really bonded as a family, and everyone looked at me like a father figure or an older brother. Especially after having chosen me to be the preacher of our home, they opened up to me a lot more.

One evening, while David and I were busy with a project, he asked the wildest question I had ever heard. He inquired if I would consider marrying him and Alli. I was completely taken aback. "What, when, how did this come about? I mean, I would be flattered, but when did you propose to Alli, and how long have you two been together?"

David smiled and mentioned that they had been together since roughly the time we discovered the old, deserted warehouse. "Losing Josh and Mary made me understand that life is fleeting; I had always been fond of Alli, but I never found the courage to ask her out. Therefore, I concluded that it was now or never." I took my dad's advice to heart: "A moment of courage can lead to a lifetime of change."

I inquired whether they had settled on a date for their wedding. He replied with a quick "Yes!"

That must have been the quickest wedding ever organized. Within three days, our bunker was completely transformed, turning into a stunning garden filled with flowers and handmade decorations.

I'm not sure how it happened, but Alli managed to find a lovely dress for herself along with a sports jacket and bow tie for David. They looked stunning together. I was really happy they had chosen me to officiate their wedding. I had never married anyone before, and I never would have imagined doing something like that in a million years. Yet I also never thought I would have baptized anyone or completed all the things we had done up to that moment.

Jed was the one who had dreamed of becoming a preacher, not me. Not only is God amazing, but He also has a huge sense of humor. It's amazing what He can achieve not just in your life but also through you to bless others when you fully give your heart to Him. One lesson I've learned during my short journey with Him is that the greatest blessing comes from blessing others through our obedience.

Jasmine had found an acoustic guitar in the house before the fire. It had likely belonged to either Jed or his grandfather, but we were thankful to have it. During her military deployment in Okinawa, Japan, Jasmine had picked up a few chords.

That evening, as we celebrated David and Alli's wedding, Jasmine played several well-loved songs that everyone enjoyed. We were having a fantastic time. We even arranged a special meal and organized some games for later.

Out of nowhere, we were startled by the most deafening sound we had ever encountered. It resembled a mix of thunder and a tornado simultaneously. The earth trembled fiercely, and this went on for several hours. We speculated it could be a storm or an earthquake, but what we discovered was even more alarming.

We realized we were right in the thick of the tribulation, but we weren't quite sure how it would impact us. When we switched on the radio, what we heard next hit us hard. Reports came in that thousands, maybe even millions, of creatures had suddenly materialized. They seemed to be some kind of beings riding horses that resembled fiery lions.

These entities were very well organized with one clear goal: to eliminate anyone and anything that came into their view. This powerful force was the same army referenced in the ninth chapter of the book of Revelation.

Despite knowing that only heartbreaking news was being reported day after day, we found it impossible to resist the temptation to tune in; we felt compelled to stay informed about unfolding events.

Numerous people suffered at the hands of these entities. Global reports showed that both those who were marked and those who were not faced violent attacks.

What next? We wondered what would happen next outside in the world, and what would happen to us. Although death could have come at any moment during these difficult days, we all felt we had an unshakable peace.

We learned to find contentment in every situation we faced, whether good or bad, as we firmly believed that Christ was always with us. If we were to keep living on this earth, we chose to live for Christ; and if we were to die, it would be for our gain.

COMMITTED

Zoe and Jubilee, the twins, made an important choice to dedicate their lives to Christ. This decision wasn't just a response to their current circumstances; it arose from a profound desire that had been developing in their hearts for a long time. Nevertheless, they struggled with doubts regarding the actions they should take to honor this commitment.

Even though their mother had been a dedicated Christian for quite a while, she never truly explained to them what it meant to accept Christ. I think she always assumed the girls understood it automatically.

Their father, in contrast, was never one to attend church; he had always held the belief that you shape your own destiny. He thought that if you led a good life, you would eventually enjoy the fruits of your labor; but if you lived poorly, then the outcome would be different.

The girls mentioned that immediately following the vanishings, their father was extremely upset with God because their mother had disappeared. However, over time he came to understand that his wife had gently warned him repeatedly, but he never truly believed her until a year after she was gone.

The twins were eager to accept Christ as their Savior. They asked me to guide them in a prayer to make sure they prayed correctly. I was more than happy to pray with them and for them.

They wanted to be baptized right away, so the crew and I filled a storage tub with water. I felt privileged to baptize those lovely ladies who, at this point, had grown to be like my daughters. Interestingly, Jasmine felt the same way about them.

After David and Alli got married, I thought about it all the time. It had never crossed my mind before, especially with the apocalypse happening around us. But for some reason, I never realized it until the twins' baptism—I've always had a thing for Jasmine.

I took some time to think about the advice David's dad had shared with him, and I concluded that being late is better than never getting there. With that in mind, I approached

Jasmine and asked if we could have a private chat.

She gave me a smile. "What do you want?"

I was so nervous. Maybe I hadn't really thought this through. The next words, or whatever came out of my mouth, could have been in a different language altogether.

Jasmine laughed and said, "Just go for it!"

"All right, here it is. Jasmine, would you want to be my girlfriend?"

"Wow, finally! I thought you'd never ask! Did it really take the end of the world for you to notice me, Richard?"

"Well, no," I said. "I noticed you back in high school, but I figured you wouldn't be into me."

"You silly, I noticed you in high school too!"

Wow! All right! "So does that mean you'll be my girlfriend?"

"Absolutely, my answer is yes!" Jasmine answered. "But I have a question for you, Richard! When are we getting married?"

I hadn't seen that coming, but I answered her anyway. Without really thinking, I just said, "Soon," to which Jasmine replied, "Okay."

That evening, we were all incredibly happy that those beings could have come, found us, and taken us away; I would have still died the happiest man on earth!

It was disheartening that as we celebrated the wonderful things the Lord was doing in our lives, people were losing their lives every single day. I truly believe that the most important thing we could have done during that period was to pray. We prayed for everyone, both those who were marked and those who were not.

It had been some time since we last heard from Cohen. Following the arrival of these creatures and the onset of the attacks, there was little news about him.

One morning, as we tuned into the OWGO broadcast, Cohen chose to speak to the world. He started, as was his custom, by saying, "My beloved children."

"I understand we have encountered very dangerous times, but rest assured, I have battled these creatures and put an end to them.

"Under my leadership, the OWFP has triumphed over these beings that plagued us for more than five months. To all of you who have endured and stayed loyal to me, brighter days are now ahead."

The broadcast further elaborated that Cohen had plans to gather a formidable force of two hundred million individuals from multiple countries. His objective was to lead a military operation designed to ultimately defeat his adversary.

Regardless of the circumstances, our intention was to stay devoted to the Lord. We faced tough times, and each day we braced ourselves for something even more outrageous, yet we chose not to live in fear but to hold on to the hope that one day we would be united with Him in paradise.

chapter eight

WAITING

"I wait for the Lord, my soul waits, And in His word I do hope."

PSALM 130:5

It had been a few months since Cohen revealed his plan. The atmosphere was eerily calm—almost *too* calm, if you asked me. We sensed that something was on the horizon, but we had no idea just how severe it would turn out to be.

We really tried our best to live a normal life, following our daily routine that involved work, having fun, and doing our daily devotional. We remembered a Bible verse that highlighted the significance of being faithful and putting down roots wherever God has put us. This message struck a chord with us, reminding us that our dedication to our current circumstances was crucial, as it honored God.

We got some amazing news from David and Alli—they were having a baby! Wow, a little one coming into all this chaos. That's what I thought anyway. But no matter what, that baby was going to be a blessing for everyone. Hearing news like that felt great. It gave us a spark of hope in the midst of darkness.

THE PLAN

One sunny afternoon, Jasmine, Justice, and I were having a great time in the garden when we suddenly heard the buzzing of a few drones flying close by. Although we couldn't see them, we felt their presence in the air. Realizing there was no way to escape them, we quickly came up with a plan that eventually led to our rescue.

Close by, there was a little creek with an undercut, I figured it would be a great idea to run over to the creek and hide. It would keep us out of sight from the drones until they left.

We reached the undercut and spent a solid hour underneath it. When we finally emerged, we felt like two soggy noodles. Even Justice, who usually loves the water, felt damp.

When we arrived at the Ark, everyone was curious about what had happened to us. They were concerned that we might have been caught by the OWFP, as they also had heard the drones.

Returning home felt so peaceful. After going through that terrifying ordeal, I realized I needed to reevaluate my life. So I took a leap of faith and asked Jasmine if she would marry me right then and there.

She looked at me and answered, "Yes! Let's do it tomorrow; that way, we can decorate the bunker and pick out some lovely outfits for our wedding."

I was fine with that; tomorrow seemed just as good as any day. However, I was really looking forward to it—just the thought of marrying Jasmine the next day lifted my spirits immensely.

The following morning, everyone got up early. The twins, in particular, jumped on my bunk and exclaimed, "It's time, silly! It's time for your wedding!"

Oh right, my wedding! I turned to the guys and said,

"All right, I totally forgot one thing. Who's going to officiate?"

"I am, knucklehead!" David chimed in. "Need I remind you who baptized you?" So then, we are all set!

Everyone was filled with excitement, and everything was ready. Then, out from behind the curtain came Jasmine. Wow, she looked stunning; all I could say was, "Wow! How did you girls pull off such beauty?"

The twins replied, "Love, that's all it takes—love."

"Well, I appreciate everything, everyone! Let's get this started, Dave!"

Believe it or not, the ceremony was beautiful; David did a fantastic job officiating our marriage. Afterward, the twins performed a song for us, and even Jeremiah and Sarah joined in the singing.

I wouldn't have changed a single thing. That was the most wonderful wedding I have ever attended. I might be a bit biased, since it was my own wedding, but the warmth and love in the room—or should I say, the bunker—truly made everything shine.

A couple of months after our wedding, just as everything seemed to be going well and everyone was busy doing their daily activities, the earth suddenly started to shake with a fierceness that surpassed even the chaos of a stampede of thousands of horses. The ground quaked violently, causing trees to fall all around us, creating a scene of utter destruction. It became abundantly clear that it was far too dangerous to remain outdoors during this terrifying event.

Everyone had arrived safely at the bunker, or so we thought. I glanced around and noticed that Jubilee was missing. I asked Zoe, "Where's your sister?"

She replied, "I don't know." She appeared quite frightened. Jasmine then said, "I think she went down to the creek; it was her turn to do the laundry."

Without a second thought, I sprinted as quickly as possible toward the creek. It wasn't easy; the ground continued to tremble, and trees were still crashing down. At that moment, nothing else mattered to me—all I could focus on was reaching my little girl.

When I arrived at the creek, I couldn't locate Jubilee. Just as despair was setting in, I prayed to God, saying, "Please Lord, don't take her away. Help me find her." Right after I finished my prayer, Justice started barking a short distance down the creek.

I hurried to the location where Justice was, and to my shock, I discovered Jubilee lying unconscious in the water. Thankfully, she was positioned face up, which was a relief because if she had been facing down, the situation could have been far more dire.

It appears that while she was washing some clothes, a branch fell from a tree and struck her on the head. This unexpected incident caused her to lose consciousness and fall into the creek.

I'm really grateful to our Lord that Justice had tagged along and that we'd made it there just in time. If we had taken even a little longer, the water could have flipped Jubilee over, and that might have created a drowning hazard.

As I lifted Jubilee out of the water, I thanked God and praised Justice for being a good boy. I then checked to see if she was breathing, and thankfully, she was. I hurried back to the bunker with her in my arms, and Justice trailed closely behind us.

When we arrived at the Ark, everyone was thrilled to see Jubilee. They immediately asked what had happened, and I shared all the details with everyone. Right away, David and Jasmine jumped in to provide first aid.

Jubilee bounced back quickly; the injury she had was not as severe as we initially feared. She, along with everyone else, was reminded not to venture out alone, as it was crucial for everyone to go out in pairs.

The earthquake caused significant destruction in our region. However, the most extensive damage occurred near the OWGO compound. The earthquake registered above a magnitude 10, and its impact was felt globally. There had never been an earthquake of that magnitude, leading to numerous fatalities and widespread devastation.

Cohen quickly declared a worldwide emergency. Without delay, he summoned all global leaders and convinced them that it was essential to unite their military might to face and finally vanquish Christ once and for all.

He blamed God for the countless deaths and devastation that had taken place. He announced to the world that God was evil and had to be eradicated at any price.

Cohen commanded an army of two hundred million, and his strategy was to personally wage war against God, aiming to conquer Him at Armageddon. He further stated that once his forces triumphed over God, the Christians would also be eliminated.

UNDERGROUND

A number of our projects needed to be reconstructed, including the garden. Fortunately, our bunker was spared from any damage. The old barn was completely destroyed, which meant we had to use the tunnel entrance in the wooded area to enter and exit.

Jasmine and I were on our way home one evening after foraging in an area where we had discovered a variety of edible items. Suddenly, an elderly woman emerged from behind a tree, her hands raised in a gesture of peace. She reassured us, saying, "Don't be afraid; I'm not here to harm you."

We were terrified; it had been ages since we had encountered anyone. Without hesitation, I pulled out my weapon and aimed it at her, demanding to know who she was and what her intentions were. She replied, "We come in peace. My husband and I would like to invite you to our underground church."

"Underground church? What do you mean by that, ma'am? And where is your husband?"

Out of nowhere, we heard a voice call out, "Hello, young ones, I'm up here." The elderly man—her spouse—was perched in a tree with a rifle aimed at us. She remarked, "If we'd wanted to harm you, we would have done it by now."

She went on to say, "We are unmarked and followers of Christ. We've been watching you for some time, but we didn't want to alarm you."

"What has changed now?" I replied.

"The earthquake. We wanted to ensure that you and your group are safe and have enough food."

We had so many questions, and to be frank, we did not trust them at all. Nevertheless, Jasmine and I chose to dig a bit deeper. We trailed behind the elderly woman, who called herself Linda, and her husband as they took us on a roundabout path to their home; it likely took around an hour.

They guided us to a hill with a hidden door. Upon our arrival, we were in awe. From the exterior, it was impossible to discern that the door was an entrance. The most astonishing moment came when we stepped inside. A staircase led us down below. Once we reached the bottom, we discovered a small community residing there, each family having their own bunker, all linked to a larger communal space where they gathered.

They showed us countless rows of corn and different veggies grown underground. Jasmine and I were honestly shocked, to say the least. They invited us to sit down, and the older man introduced himself as Pastor James. He told us his whole story, revealing that he had been a scientist for the government before the disappearances and how he had been building and preparing this for many years, mentioning that he had seen the signs a long time ago.

The community primarily consisted of his children, grandchildren, and other families who had also attended the same church as him. None of them had accepted the mark, and James mentioned that he had been avoiding his true calling until this moment. He extended an invitation for us to join them, whether to live with them or simply to visit and participate in their church services, which took place every Sunday.

They seemed like good people, but we still had some doubts about fully trusting them. What put my mind at ease was his readiness to let us keep our weapons, showing that he meant no harm.

When we returned to our bunker, the rest of our group was really worried about us and curious about our whereabouts. We shared everything that had happened, and they were in disbelief at what they were hearing. The twins were super excited, along with Jeremiah and Sarah, and they wanted to know if we were going that coming Sunday. David and I devised a plan, just in case they intended to harm us after all.

Sunday arrived fast; Jasmine and I chose to just bring the girls this time. David would stay nearby but wouldn't join us inside. It was a bit of a gamble, but it was better than having no plan whatsoever. Our desire for community was so strong that we pushed aside our feelings of distrust. On the flip side, if they turned out to be good people, we could make new friends and brothers in Christ.

The moment we got there, they swung open the secret door for us like they had been expecting us all along. Everyone greeted us warmly. It felt almost unreal. The twins were ecstatic; they enjoyed every second of it. There were quite a few other kids around their age.

They led us into the main area. This time, there were rows of chairs arranged neatly and a pulpit with a Bible set up for Sunday service. When they started, they sang a few gospel songs, which were beautiful. The sermon delivered by Pastor James was spot on: a message that came straight from the heart of God.

The longer we hung out with them, the more we understood that they weren't trying to harm us; they were genuinely like us. They also yearned for community and were eager to share their blessings. After the sermon, they brought out a bunch of plates filled with food and treats they had made. We really enjoyed the time together afterward.

As we were leaving, Pastor James said, "Next time, bring all your friends—and let the young man who's been hanging around outside know that he should come in too."

Surprised, I asked, "How did you know?" He clarified that not *all* the drones were part of the OWFP.

When we returned to the Ark, the rest of our crew was eager to hear all about our experience with the new community, which we decided to call "the hill."

The twins were very excited to talk about the amazing experience they just had. It felt like they were discovering the world all over again with fresh eyes. Honestly, we felt the same way too.

Before we knew it, one Sunday turned into many. We really enjoyed going to the hill; it made life feel normal again. Pastor James; his wife, Linda; and the rest of the hill community were amazing. They offered us more than just their food; they shared their hearts and love. We had nearly forgotten that we were right in the middle of the end of the world.

ARMAGEDDON

The moment arrived for Cohen and his troops to gather at the field of Megiddo. Every action was being transmitted over the radio and shown on TV too. One cool thing about the hill was that Pastor James somehow got a TV signal without anyone being able to detect it. We could watch everything happening through a projector and screen he had arranged for his community.

This was such a treat; we hadn't seen any kind of TV or screen in ages. The hill also had a bunch of family movies that we all enjoyed watching. One of the coolest things about movie night was the popcorn. Yep, popcorn! That was quite a shock to us.

That's why it was tough to say no when Pastor James and the hill community asked us to stay with them permanently. At least, not just yet. We really enjoyed our time with the hill community, but there was something unique about our little bunker: It felt like home. Jed and his family had sacrificed so much to leave that for us. We just couldn't bring ourselves to leave our home behind.

We kept visiting every other Sunday and sometimes on Fridays for movie night. But when Jeremiah and Sarah asked if they could live in the hill community full-time, we told them it was really up to them. We didn't mind at all; we would miss them, but the good news was that they were just a hop, skip, and a jump away.

The hill community really turned into a strong support system for our family. David and Alli started relying on this community even more, especially after their son, Josiah, was born.

There, Josiah had other children to play with, and the hill also provided a school-like atmosphere where the little one could learn and develop. I was truly delighted for both David and Alli.

As for us and the girls, we kept living at the Ark and made occasional trips to the hill. The girls enjoyed their visits, but at the end of the day it was nice to have our own place to return to. Not to mention, Justice appreciated the extra space he had; he even got his own bunk bed now. We missed the rest of our crew, but we found comfort in knowing they weren't too far away.

We made every effort to visit our family on the hill whenever possible. Everyone could feel that something significant was approaching. We had encountered various challenges before, but this time it seemed different. Instead of fear, though, we simply felt that time was running out.

We approached every day as though it were our final one. We loved deeper, we savored life more, and regardless of what we witnessed or listened to, we focused our thoughts on Christ and His Word.

If you had asked me a few years back whether I saw

myself as a religious person, I would have thought you were out of your mind. Even now, I don't view myself as a religious individual. Instead, I see myself as a man of God: I love God wholeheartedly.

In a peculiar way, I wouldn't have changed anything that transpired. All the experiences we faced made me stronger and more genuine, not just in my relationship with God but also toward others and life as a whole.

That evening, we experienced a few slight tremors, so the following morning we chose to spend the day at the hill. Upon our arrival, we found they had just completed breakfast and were preparing to begin their daily devotional. They inquired if we were hungry, and we replied that we had already eaten. However, the girls had different thoughts and requested if they could have some breakfast.

Following our devotional, Pastor James requested that we include everything occurring in the outside world in our prayers. He noted that situations were intensifying and expressed his belief that we would soon be witnessing the return of our Lord.

Tensions were rising in the Valley of Megiddo. Cohen had intensified the animosity toward God and incited all the global leaders. If I hadn't witnessed it myself, I wouldn't have believed what was unfolding.

The view at Megiddo was surreal; it seemed like a scene from a film. The hatred toward God and the unmarked was palpable through the radio and television signals. Every day, they would shout against God, cursing Him and challenging Him to show Himself if He truly existed.

A variety of tanks, armored vehicles, and weapons were positioned, prepared to battle against our God. What was Cohen thinking? How could he believe that he could not only oppose Him but also overcome Him?

This act could only have been committed by a crazed individual who had completely lost his grip on reality. The worst part was that he had somehow managed to convince everyone that they could triumph over the Lord of lords and the King of kings.

FAITHFUL

In those last days, the OWGO ramped up its search for the unmarked. Drones flew through the skies every day. The time was almost upon us—the time when our Lord Jesus will come back. We felt a blend of excitement and a hint of fear as we confronted the unknown of what truly was to come.

Our Lord was returning, not just to defeat Satan and

deliver judgment on everyone who had turned away from Him by accepting the mark but also to set up His kingdom right here on earth.

The toughest part was the waiting; still, we understood that waiting required trust. We had faith in His Word, convinced that He was faithful and would fulfill what He had promised would come.

Jed's note indicated that the end was approaching quickly. He mentioned in his writings that when we witness the anti-Christ gathering an army against God at the Valley of Megiddo we should look up, as our redemption was close at hand.

Jed's last journal entry mentioned that after this, it wouldn't take long for the A-Team to come back together. We had to keep our faith and trust in God. He ended by saying he loved us and looked forward to seeing us soon! Those words brought us comfort and hope. We remained faithful as we continued to trust in God.

Even with all the chaos around us, our lives stayed steady. We kept on working and building. More importantly, we kept getting closer to each other and to Christ. His Word made us strong. While we waited, we could relate to how the disciples must have felt, waiting for the promise of the Holy

Spirit in the upper room.

Despite the OWFP increasing their surveillance, we maintained our faith in the Lord and continued to meet with our brothers and sisters at the hill. We remained steadfast in prayer and our connection with them. Our dedication to seeking God in the face of challenges resulted in many miracles occurring among us. Additionally, numerous brothers and sisters were being baptized. God was truly moving in our lives.

The upgraded drones that OWGO had introduced were truly unique. Their advanced technology made them undetectable. They operated silently and were invisible to the naked eye. However, that didn't prevent us from visiting our family in the hill. We stayed loyal to our Lord and to one another.

One evening, while we were making our way back to the Ark, a booming voice echoed from the sky, instructing us to halt and refrain from running. Out of nowhere, a swarm of the drones materialized, encircling us completely. We were certain that our fate was sealed.

What transpired next was entirely all God's doing; we had already given up, fully aware that there was no way out. The drones continued to issue orders for us to stay put. From out of nowhere they began to ascend, directing someone or something away from us to halt and refrain from fleeing. We were left puzzled about who they were pursuing, as we couldn't see anyone ahead of them.

They returned to the spot where we were, yet for some strange reason they couldn't see us; it felt as though we had become invisible to them. We were in disbelief, even standing up and waving at them, but there was no response, as if we had disappeared.

We decided to head back to the hill, since it was closer than our bunker at that moment. When we got there, Pastor James asked what had happened while swiftly leading us inside.

Everyone was glad to have us back at the hill, safe and sound; Jeremiah and Sarah greeted us with a big hug, thanking God for our safety. Even Justice was excited to be surrounded by all our friends and family.

Pastor James expressed his happiness that we returned, mentioning that conditions were deteriorating outside as he gestured toward the screen displaying all nations assembled at Megiddo. He then invited everyone to join in prayer. In the heart of the complex, we came together and prayed in unity. We all felt the impending events.

After all that we had been through, after all the challenges we faced, we felt that it would soon come to an end. It was hard to believe. While we were praying, we could hear the live broadcast; in the background, we could hear Cohen laughing and challenging God as he marched across the Valley at Megiddo with his army of two hundred million.

Out of nowhere, a powerful gust of wind swept through, accompanied by the loud sound of a trumpet blast. Moreover, the unmistakable noise of a whole army of horses galloping could be heard, their hooves striking the ground in a booming beat.

As we all stared intently at the screen, a brilliant white light suddenly erupted, lighting up the room before the screen went dark. A strange silence surrounded us, and in that instant, we instinctively understood what had just occurred. Our redeemer had arrived.

Victory!

They triumphed over him by the blood of the Lamb and by the word of their testimony; they did not love their lives so much as to shrink from death.

REVELATION 12:11

About the Author

David Mendoza III is a dedicated servant leader with a rich tapestry of experience spanning faith, service, and storytelling. Holding a seminary degree in biblical studies, he brings a deep understanding of faith and Scripture to his work. A retired federal law enforcement officer with over thirty years of service, David has dedicated his life to protecting and serving others. His military background as a Marine Corps veteran further underscores his commitment to duty and resilience.

David's passion for helping others extends beyond his professional life. He has served as a law enforcement chaplain, a peer support member, and a Veterans Support Program volunteer, offering guidance and support to those in need. Currently, David is a Christian minister and former pastor, sharing his faith and wisdom through his ministry.

He is the author of several award-winning books, including *Unleashed Redemption* and *The King & His Bride*, and a variety of captivating children's titles such as *The Biblical Adventures of Floppy and Hoppy*, *Gideon the Brave Bulldog*, *Wheezy & Goliath*, *A Lemon-flavored Popsicle*, *K9 Rudie: The Service Dog*, *Hero Bunny*, and *Don't Hang Around Turkeys*, all of which bring biblical narratives to life for young audiences.

David's life is a testament to the power of faith, service, and storytelling. He is a devoted husband of over thirty years, a father of two boys, and an active member of his church community, where he and his wife are deeply involved in adult and children's ministry. David's unwavering commitment to helping others, sharing his testimony, and offering support during times of need makes him a true inspiration.

David is reachable via email at *authordavidmendozaiii@yahoo.com*, or you can visit his website at *www.booksforhisglory.com* to get in touch.

www.ingramcontent.com/pod-product-compliance
Lightning Source LLC
Chambersburg PA
CBHW050451110726
47899CB00003B/897
* 9 7 9 8 9 9 2 2 1 3 4 5 4 *